River's Journey

by

Ryan Jo Summers

Winds of Destiny, Book 1

River's Journey

Contact Information: info@thewildrosepress.com

Cover Art by *Abigail Owen*

The Wild Rose Press, Inc.
PO Box 708
Adams Basin, NY 14410-0708
Visit us at www.thewildrosepress.com

Publishing History
First Sweetheart Rose Edition, 2021
Trade Paperback ISBN 978-1-5092-3501-8
Digital ISBN 978-1-5092-3502-5

Winds of Destiny, Book 1
Published in the United States of America

"Are you telling me you would never marry a man if it were just mutually beneficial between you? Is that what you are implying?" he challenged her, bringing his palms back to the tabletop.

She shook her head, moving tangled hair out of the way. "No, I would only marry for true love and nothing less."

He envied her confident answer. Yet, it explained why this tumultuous woman was still single. However, his curiosity won out. "Okay, and what do you consider nothing less than true love?" Was there even such a thing?

She smiled.

Her smile was the first real smile he'd seen from her. Almost dreamy, it slammed into his chest with all the tenderness of a bulldozer. He counted the seconds until he could force a shallow breath back into his lungs. One...two...three...four...five... Would she ever answer him?

"That's hard to put into words. It's more something two people will feel when destiny speaks, and they are the right two."

He could have almost laughed, if he had been able to breathe properly. "Then you think it's destiny that makes two people fall in love?"

"No. I think destiny brings them together. They fall in love because they are meant to."

Ah, crystal clear, considering it was coming from her. "Well, that is an interesting point of view, I suppose." He brushed off any crumbs that might be on the table or stuck in the scarred ridges. "However, my arrangement with Miss Jordon is my business and none of yours, so kindly keep your opinions to yourself."

Praise for Ryan Jo Summers

"I did greatly enjoy the read and see you leading into Storm's story!"

~ Leslie Maier

~*~

"One of the best authors in the genre - I have looked forward to the publication of her latest book!"

~Carol M.

Dedication

This story is dedicated
to all the people who call themselves dreamers.
We daydream to make it through our day;
we dream at night of happy things.
We chase our dreams and long to catch them.
Thank you for picking up my daydream.
Sweetwater Harbor was birthed in my mind as a happy
place to escape the realities of an unhappy day job.
Over time, people came to town
and found their own dreams waiting
on Sweetwater Harbor's sandy shores.
May you—dear reader—find all your dreams
and hold them tight.

Chapter One

The old man was dying. He knew it without the solemn stares coming from the doctor and the nurses. Before he parted, he had one more bit of unfinished business. This last, important task was one he should have attended to a long time ago. He smiled grimly as he looked into the worried faces of his two friends and neighbors of the last thirty-two years. "Call my son," he requested. His tone was mild, but his eyes told of his urgency.

Muriel and Cordell Gallagher exchanged glances, their brows furrowing equally. Muriel cleared her throat and then reached for her husband's hand before speaking. "And what of River?"

"Call her, too. Nothing changes for her, but I need to discuss things." He blew out a shaky breath. "Then call for Calder."

"As you wish, Frank," Cordell promised as he lifted a questioning eyebrow. "If you are sure."

He nodded, looking across the room at an abstract painting of reds and yellows. "No way any of us can know how this will end, but I know how I want it to finish."

****

Calder Finn stood on the eighth hole of the Vista Views Golf Club, just north of Atlanta, Georgia, studying the slope and enjoying the warm sunshine on

1

his face. His best friend and business partner, Brody McGee, and two of their business clients were taking full advantage of March's first nice day to shoot a few holes and discuss a little work.

So far, Calder was winning by a landslide. He'd had a great week, the weekend looked promising, and he could not be happier. He just made up his mind to use the nine iron for this shot and reached for it when his phone rang.

Now, why hadn't he remembered to put it on vibrate? Well, too late now. It would just ring until voice mail kicked in. "Sorry. I forgot about it." He reached for the phone. "Just let me handle this quickly so we can get back to the game." Without glancing at the number, he issued a neutral greeting.

"Calder? This is Cordell Gallagher. From Sweetwater Harbor."

At the names, he went cold. Squeezing his eyes tight, he clenched his hand around the phone in a white-knuckled grip. His mouth dried. *Sweetwater Harbor.* Memories swamped him despite the warm Georgia sunshine. "Yes." He struggled to voice the single word despite his tongue felt like it turned to rubber.

His windpipe constricted in a painful vise. He tightened his fingers around the golf club. Without asking, he knew what this call was about. Forcing in a shaky breath, he turned from Brody and the men.

"It's your dad, Calder. You need to come back home now."

****

Calder gritted his teeth, reining in his impatience. This endless hassle was exactly why he seldom went back to Sweetwater Harbor. He was certain getting there from here was impossible. Not without a whole lot of aggravation and extra steps. He stared at the pile of notes and pen resting beside the phone, heaved a heavy sigh, let his gaze sweep the living room, and came back to the pages of notes and directions. Briefly, he considered plowing his arm through the whole mess to send it flying across the room.

Then, he inhaled a deep breath and clutched the pen again. Damn, but he would get these travel plans figured out how to go from Atlanta to Sweetwater Harbor in one day. The trip wasn't all that long in miles, but the town was just a little backwater settlement so far off the beaten path.

His brow puckered as he mapped out the last leg of his plan to fulfill his father's dying wish. Returning home really should not be this difficult. But it was. If he didn't know better, he would take the travel difficulties to indicate he wasn't meant to return. No going back. Never returning had been his plan years ago, when he left Sweetwater Harbor in the dust of his rearview mirror. Except in the dark recesses of his mind, he'd always known this time would arrive one day. He just hadn't expected it so soon.

He studied the lengthy list and blew out another frustrated breath. Okay, first, the flight from Atlanta, Georgia, to Raleigh, North Carolina, which wasn't too bad. Then he'd hop on a smaller connection to Lady Beth, the next town on his journey. Smaller. He grimaced. Probably not much better than, and akin to, a crop duster. He could easily picture the airplane as a single-engine, one-propeller kind of machine. Then in Lady Beth, he'd rent a car and make the two-and-a-half-hour drive to Sweetwater Harbor.

Then…well, then the rest of his journey would be all downhill.

****

River Gallagher left Frank Finn's house and turned her car toward her parents, who lived at the next house down from the end of Finn Summit. As neighbors and friends in Sweetwater Harbor for longer than she'd been alive, she knew Frank's long illness and dismal prognosis was hard on them, too. She'd known this time would eventually come, but just knowing the facts didn't make accepting those facts easier. The drive took only moments, and she paused in the driveway to stare out at the rolling waves of the Atlantic Ocean as the breakers rushed onto the sandy shore. Seagulls and boats dotted the blue water and cloudless sky. Today, the familiar sight was wholly soothing.

She adored Frank Finn like a second father, and they shared many of the same ideas and philosophies. Not like his only child, Calder. Perhaps, he was the crux of her unsettled emotions? Before long she would have to work with Calder Finn in a business deal—if he returned. Dad only said he'd not sounded very happy when he called him in Georgia, not that Calder would commit to making the trip back. Knowing what her immediate future held regarding Calder's plans and his whereabouts would go a long way to settle her nerves.

Arriving at her parents' house, River threw her electric car into Park, grabbed her pocketbook, and headed for the steps. While she absently looked at the familiar sights and sounds of the beachfront home, she slowed her steps to think about Calder, who once had been the boy next door. What did she really know about him?

River barely remembered him. Four years ahead of her in school, he'd left almost immediately after graduation, while she finished with her freshman year. By the time she was dating boys, he was just a memory Frank spoke of at times. To judge by Frank's opinions, she and Calder would have little in common anyway.

Her shoes clunked along the wooden boards of the deck as she made her way to the door. She knocked first before entering with a shout of welcome. In Sweetwater Harbor, every expected guest behaved this way. Such arrival was considered normal. What would Calder think once he returned and realized how his dad set up his estate? She grinned. If he returned, he was in for a few surprises and adjustments.

****

Calder frowned as he drove his rental car through town. Nothing had changed in the fourteen years he'd been gone. During his long drive to the coast, he passed towns that were developed—many along the coast capitalizing on the scenic beachfront property. He drove by housing communities and healthy commerce. Until now.

In Sweetwater Harbor, he saw a ridiculously small black spot—a dot on a map that had not yet joined the twenty-first century. The dot proved how his father encouraged the lack of growth to keep Sweetwater Harbor in the past.

Slowing the car, he crossed the drawbridge and glanced around, shaking his head in wonder. Here, time stood still. The area was void of high-rise hotels or five-star restaurants. The Newport Diner still stood on the same corner as it had years ago. The church, the hardware store, barber and beauty shop, and grocery store remained where they were when he left. The only difference was a few buildings might be sporting a new coat of paint. Even the signs were the same, for crying out loud.

He coasted by Turn the Page Bookstore and paused. Well, at least that business was something new. He eyed the small storefront nestled between the hardware store and post office.

Perhaps now he could do something with this little berg, since he'd just inherited most of this dot on the map. He'd bring modern blood to these ancient spaces. A plan formed in his mind. He could scout around, create some solid ideas while he liquefied his dad's assets, and then get out of town as fast as possible, returning to Atlanta. He had an important personal affair there coming up soon, and he still had a business to run. Good grief, he had a life waiting back there. Here, everywhere he looked was nothing but memories and headaches.

Once he returned home, he would send a team from the firm here and let them do the actual groundwork. He would set everything up so he only had to return when absolutely necessary. He and Brody employed enough competent workers in the firm who would love to come spend time at the Carolina beach. They'd think they were getting a real deal. A smile tugged on his face for the first time since he'd arrived in town as he mulled the plan over. This idea could be perfect, and he'd never let on how much aggravation they saved him during their little beach-cation.

Sure of his strategy, he turned the rental car down Finn's Summit to the biggest house at the end of the street—his dad's house. His house now.

He'd start by checking around the house. No telling what shape it was in by now. He parked and stood by the car, breathing in the cold salt air blowing off the ocean as he stared up at the three-story house, seeming larger than he remembered. Sea grass and sea oats danced in the breeze, waving almost as if to welcome his return. The cool air slapped his cheeks. He'd also forgotten the sharp scent of salt and pines, and how cold the weather—and the air—was here in March.

Stuffing his hands in his pockets, he headed for the house. First, he'd check the strength of the support beams that supported the house. Then he would examine the levels of stairs and decking before he worked his way to the windows and doors. He needed to know exactly what condition his place was in.

****

River paced to the window overlooking her parent's yard and glanced out at the tide washing ashore. Behind her, she sensed her parent's patience, giving her some much-needed time to work out her feelings. Unquestionably, everyone in town knew Frank's imminent passing would be hard on her, as she was the one closest to him. Certainly, they knew she would handle the business affairs as he had asked. However, they must be worried how she would cope with the loss of such a like-minded and trusted friend. She wanted to be with him now, but she respected his desire for a little peace to take care of what he was calling his final personal business. Since it was business, she felt she needed to be with him, assisting, except he was adamant he needed to handle this alone.

She'd give him another half hour then she'd return.

"I completely agree the properties should stay the

same," she murmured, returning to her dad's comment of moments before. "Too many people in town depend—" Her fingers clasped the windowsill, and as she spotted human movement outside the window, she gasped. "Someone's over there. At Frank's." She pressed her face closer to the cool glass and squinted across the sand. "A man, and he's poking around under the house." Whirling, she faced her dad as he slowly rose from the sofa. She crossed the floor and gently touched his wrist. "I'll go look, Dad. If it's some riffraff, I'll run him off."

"River—" Muriel rose from her chair. She moved as though to intercept River before she made it to the door.

"I'll be careful, Mom. I'll even take Storm's baseball bat from the garage, okay? You know I am both capable and willing to club someone, if needed."

"We'll be watching from the window," Muriel nodded. She cast a look outside, then rolled a button on her blouse. "If you need help, just wave. We shall send in the cavalry."

River smiled, picturing her sixty-something parents rushing across the sand to her aid. "Promise." She stalked downstairs, paused long enough to grab her sister's baseball bat, and then headed toward Frank Finn's property. She was glad she was in shoes and pants today. Gliding across the loose ground came easier in flats than heels and a skirt would allow. The wind was heavy with the scent of dotted horsemint and Indian blanket flowers just beginning to bloom.

A dark blue car sat parked in the driveway, and she acknowledged the nice high-end make. Why would some trespassing riffraff be driving a luxury car? How much sense was that? She rounded a loblolly bay bush and spotted the intruder kicking at the support poles under the back deck. Her chest heaved and heated fury fanned through her body. Who did he think he was? Trespassing and vandalizing!

She curled her fingers around the wooden handle of the bat and brought it up, ready to swing. Quietly, she padded over the sand toward the man. He was dressed in neat, dark trousers and a herringbone sweater, and she caught sight of a striped tie looped around his neck beneath the sweater. His dark brown hair was neatly trimmed with a slight wave at the ends. Sizing up her opponent, she determined he stood at least six feet tall and carried an athletic build. Still, whoever he was, he was nothing she couldn't handle.

Plus, he had no business here, vandalizing Frank's house. Did he plan to go inside and rob the old man, too? More heated anger unfurled within her as she considered the possibility. Despite the fine clothes he wore and expensive car in the drive, River still had no guarantees to his intentions.

He kicked another beam.

She winced. Licking her lips, she swallowed and gripped the bat tight. "Hey, you!" She faced him square, the bat held aloft. "What do you think you're doing here?"

****

At the shout, Calder whirled, and his heart jumped. A woman stood a mere arm's length away, her long blonde hair blowing in the wind, a wooden club held high, and a dangerous light in her eyes. How had she sneaked up behind him? He surveyed her and inhaled a sharp breath. Brown eyes bore into his, and her expression promised she planned on using the bat. For a moment, he was torn between the unexpected woman and the weapon she held ready. Where had she come from? Taking a step forward, he caught a whiff of soft floral perfume before the salty air stole it away.

"Don't come any closer." She brought the bat back behind her shoulder and spread her legs. "Who are you, and what do you think you're doing here?"

Her stance made him think she prepared to swing. He was tempted to ask her the same thing but instead took a cautious step back. "I am checking out this house."

She frowned, the lines creasing her face.

If possible, the gesture made her look even angrier.

"Looks more like trespassing to me. And vandalism."

Calder could have almost laughed, if she didn't look like she planned to bash in his brains. What a wild beauty. With her closer now, he noticed a mole on the left side of her chin. "What business is it of yours?" He planted his feet firmly on the sand and crossed both arms over his chest. "This place isn't yours."

A fire sparked in her eyes.

His defiance was short-lived, and he took another step backward. Pretty soon, she'd have him up against the wall.

"I'm making it my business, buster." She advanced a step. "Beat it." She swung the bat once.

Calder ducked, surprised she swung. "Now, wait a minute! I own this house." He kicked through the sand and sea grass to put some distance between them and get away from the wall where she hemmed him in.

"Like the devil you do." Her lips peeled back in a

snarl. She followed her threat with another swing. "For the last time, get off this property!"

Twirling, he tripped over a shrub, landing in the sand on all fours, and scrambled to his feet. "I have a right to be here, woman!"

She advanced and swung once more.

He stumbled on the St. John's wort shrub, disbelieving she swung again. He ducked, protecting his head, as she just missed him. The air whistled past his ear, driving anger through him.

Muttering a curse, he waded in. He pulled her into a bear hug and effectively pinned her arms. Her hair swirled around him in a silky mass of blonde, momentarily blinding him. Breathing deeply, he took in her jasmine-scented shampoo. Her perfume and heat engulfed him as their hands touched, and they both fought for the bat.

She pitched against him, tossing her hair into his face and smashing her heels onto his shiny shoes. A squeal of absolute anger escaped her.

He felt her steel herself against his iron hold. Calder gritted his teeth and hung on, feeling power and anger surging through her body. He breathed in her wild scent, keenly aware of her strong, female body pulsing against his. "Would you stop it?" he ground out as he pried her fingers from the bat.

She whipped her head backward and smacked him in the jaw.

Stars danced before his vision for a moment, and he tasted blood.

"I will not! Trespasser!" she spat as she bucked against him.

He was losing the battle. Whoever she was, she had

strength and anger. "My name is Finn, and this place is mine." He emphasized the last three words. "If anyone is trespassing here, you are."

Slowly, she relaxed. Her breath came in heavy pants. She loosened her death grip on the bat and lowered it to the ground.

He released her with a fervent hope he was right in that she was giving up, and not just tricking him.

****

River stood, gasping for breath and taking in his pretty blue eyes. They looked so much like Frank's that a shiver ran over her. In fact, now that she studied him, he did resemble a younger version of Frank Finn. "Calder?" she whispered in disbelief. So, he'd come after all.

"Yes, Calder Finn." He adjusted his tie and yanked at his sweater. "Of Finn Summit. And you are?" He ran his gaze over her.

She spotted his impatient challenge. "River Gallagher." Still winded from their battle, she watched him search his memory for the name. She still felt winded from their battle. He was a strong opponent, full of solid muscle beneath his fine suit. He'd grown since he left town. The young graduate had become a man. He was no longer the gangly youngster in the photos Frank proudly displayed inside throughout the house.

"You're one of the Gallaghers from over there?" He jerked a thumb over his shoulder toward the next-door house across the sand. "I remember my parents had been friends with them, and they had some daughters. Which one are you?"

"I'm the oldest daughter. River." She touched a finger to her chest, not quite willing to offer him her hand. What else did he remember? His stony expression said nothing. "So, you came to see your dad?"

Calder blinked, his eyes widening. "See? Well, I suppose so, though that's an odd choice of wording." He glanced up at the house, inhaled, and then turned back to her. "I'm here to settle his estate, liquefy his assets, and leave again."

A slow, wide grin crept over her face, and she watched him swallow convulsively. She nodded toward the stairs. "You'd better go inside and talk to your dad first. He has some news for you." She picked up the bat and spun around. She strode away across the sand, back home, her hair swirling behind her. Didn't he have a nice surprise waiting inside?

****

"Talk?" Calder echoed to the wind, standing dumbfounded. He'd been under the impression his dad had already passed. Of course, Cordell Gallagher had not specified, and he had not inquired. His lack of questions would serve as a hard lesson when dealing with the Gallagher clan.

He watched the wildcat, and her well-rounded backside, as she wove her way around sea oat clumps and mentally rehashed the very brief conversation he had with her father. Yes, he had assumed instead of making an educated decision. Ouch! Such an uncharacteristic mistake. He shook his head. The impulsive supposition was proof positive of his reluctance to return.

Finally, he returned his gaze and attention to the house. His dad was still alive? Not sure if it made things his plan easier or harder, he looked up to the first level. His dad was there? His heart, still racing from the skirmish with the Gallagher hellcat, skipped a few beats as he suddenly felt like a teenager coming in past curfew.

Casting one final glance at the blonde wildcat storming away, he squared his shoulders, adjusted his tie, and placed one foot on the first step. His heart thudded with uncertainties. What would he find waiting? How would his father react to his presence?

Chapter Two

"What a battle that looked like," Muriel said.

River marched through the doorway. She caught her mother's twitching grin and noticed how she avoided her dad's amused smile. River rested Storm's bat in the corner and pushed her hair behind her ears. She might need the bat again, if Calder Finn proved unreasonable. Next time, though, she would just go in swinging and forget the pleasant warnings. He could hereby consider himself warned. "That man is Calder Finn."

She sat and took the cool glass of tea her dad offered. "Seems he decided to come after all. Dad, didn't you tell him Frank was still alive?"

As Cordell returned to his chair, he lifted a shoulder in a shrug. "The lad was in a bit of a hurry to end the phone call. He asked no questions and barely let me speak more than a few sentences before he hung up." His eyebrows peaked into a snowy V. "Why? Did he draw his own conclusions?"

She nodded, swallowing deeply. The cold tea felt good on her tongue, cooling her off. Suddenly, the room was quite warm. Setting down her tea, she moved to the window overlooking the Finns' house, touching her face to the cool glass. "He seemed surprised is all," she murmured, looking out over the sand, cord grass, and yaupon bushes.

He was still there. Except now he was just standing at the front stairs, looking upward. She wished she could see his face from here. Acutely aware of each heavy heartbeat within her chest, she watched him as he tightened his silly necktie, place one hand on the banister, and begin his slow climb up the stairs. She ached to be a fly on the wall. What would Frank's reaction to his son be?

****

Calder rapped at the door once, fighting down the fluttering within his stomach. He'd been back in town less than twenty minutes and already his heart beat with unsteady palpitations. First, he'd had the wrestling match on the sand with the warrior princess next door, and then she had the gall to announce his father was alive before she sauntered off.

All right, in hindsight, perhaps he should have asked a question or two when Cordell Gallagher phoned. For example, had all his daughters turned out to be hotheaded, volatile, and beautiful as River? That information would be handy to know.

Startled at the thought, and aware his chest only fluttered more as he speculated the possibility, he knocked on the door again—a little harder this time. Not hearing anything, he tried the knob, which wasn't locked. He frowned, his hand resting uncertainly on the cold brass. Well, he recalled now not many people locked their doors in Sweetwater Harbor. "Hello? Is anyone here?" He slowly crossed the threshold, his breath held as he steeled himself. What waited for him beyond?

The big entry way was much the same as he remembered it, right down to the photos of himself and his parents on the walls. Yes, time had stood still here as well. He gave a sad shake of his head and shuffled toward the living room. "Dad?"

Rows of photos stared back at him, almost accusing him, and the memories poking him with sharp needles. He ignored them the best he could, as well as the shivers they caused to crawl up his spine. The whole place took him mentally back to when he was so anxious to escape. And now he was back. Finally, he reached the living room, lit by sunlight sparkling off the bay. Suddenly, he stopped, his breath rushing out of his lungs. "Dad?" he whispered, his throat tightening.

His dad broke into a smile, waving him into the room. "You came. I'm glad." He beckoned to a chair beside him. "Come in, son."

Son. Even the name washed memories over him, cold as the ocean outside the windows. Slowly, as he crossed the wooden floor, and he swept his gaze over his father's frail form.

At seventy-nine, he'd aged considerably since Calder was last here. Calder stood horrified as he noted the hollow look to his face and gaunt skin stretched over his bones, down to the cane resting idly at his side. Suddenly, Calder felt his legs turn to planks. He barely made it to the chair his dad indicated before he dropped heavily into it. Only his dad's blue eyes, so much like his own, seemed unchanged.

"I wasn't sure you'd come," Frank said, still beaming. "It's good to see you, son."

Calder wished he could say the same, but he could not force the words. He never expected to see his dad so gray, so old, and so thin. And so...frail. How had he aged so much? When had this happened? He dropped his gaze to the walking cane at his side, the sight conflicting with the memories of a man who could march relentlessly over sand and shore, never tiring. He wished he could ask for more, but his throat clogged. He coughed down the knot.

"Two years ago," Frank said. "Cancer. In the stomach. It spread." He patted first his belly and then a stretched-out leg. "I tried to fight it, but in the end—" He ended with a shrug of his thin shoulder.

"Two years ago?" Calder echoed, stunned that one part of time had not stood still. "Why didn't you write me? Or call? I could have—" What could he have done? Come home? Take care of his dad? Or just send him a gift basket with a get-well card? As disbelief filled him, he shook his head.

"You're here now, son. It's all that matters." Frank waved aside Calder's comment.

Yes, of course it was. Calder licked his lips and winced from the split he received from the warrior woman next door. He wished for water. Resting his hands on his knees, he fought off the impulse to adjust his tie. Brody always teased him about his nervous habit. Funny, he'd think of Brody and that running joke right now.

"You look very successful, son, in your business suit," Frank said. "I've been following your career these last years. I'm proud of you. You've done well for yourself."

Uncomfortable under his dad's sincere praise, he suddenly grew warm. He considered removing his jacket but hesitated. He turned his gaze from the old photos of him, still proudly displayed on the mantel and end tables. He swallowed the hard lump forming in his throat. "I wish I had been around. I wish I had come back occasionally." The admission did nothing to appease the guilt cutting him at the sight of his frail father.

Frank nodded. "Yes, that would have been nice. Your mother, she sure missed seeing you at the holidays."

His words, whether he intended them to or not, cut hard and went deep. Okay, so he wouldn't earn the "son of the year" award. He'd already known that.

Frank stomped his cane once. "River has been a huge help to me, though. She's kept all the properties sorted and running smoothly. That girl has been a gem."

Calder perked up. "River Gallagher?" He heard himself ask, then berated himself for asking such a stupid question. Of course, she was the very same one who only minutes ago had wanted to bash in his skull. Even now, he could smell her floral fragrance, feel her heated body fighting him, and remember the touch of her hair blowing wildly around his face.

In time, he might come to appreciate how she defended his dad with all the fury and determination of a lioness protecting her cubs. But not right now. Right now, his feet still hurt where she crushed her heels on his shoes. And he was positive his lip was split from her head knock. Again, he licked and tasted the metallic tinge of blood.

"Yes, she's such a sweet little thing." Frank smiled. "Once she grew up, turned out she was a natural at managing things. Who knew?"

Or mismanaging things, depending on one's point of view. Was the hellcat prone to making impulsive conclusions in property management like she had in this case of his identity? "You do know property management is my career in Atlanta, right, Dad?"

"Of course, I know that." Frank scoffed. "I also know Atlanta is a long way from here. How could you expect to manage a property the size we have here from all the way in Atlanta?"

Calder licked his lips and cringed again. Pretty soon he'd need lip moisturizer. A gem? Well, he was sure his dad was unable to handle his business dealings anymore. When had that change happened? He also realized his dad rather liked the little hellcat. Dread lodged in his heart. "Dad, what exactly are the arrangements you have with Miss Gallagher?"

"She is a trusted friend."

His heart skipped a beat at the leveled look in his dad's eye. "How trusted?"

He swung his skinny arm around to circle the room. "She has full governing control over everything I own."

Calder was sure his heart stopped for a few seconds. He slowly processed the words. He studied his dad, wondering if his words were some sort of bad joke. "Look, Dad, I know I've not been here. But did you have to give all that control to...River?" He barely managed to grit out her name. His dad smiled, the kind of smile one would give a dim-witted person who just asked a stupid question. To him, the question was serious.

"Why sure it was. First of all, no one can run a property like River can."

His dad's high praise made Calder wince. His hands curled into fists.

"And second, you're lucky I did not remove you from being the administrator upon my death." He stopped, shaking a thin, bony finger. "I love that sweet little girl like a daughter."

Crimson swam before Calder's eyes. He thought he might faint. Sweet? Daughter? Her? Had his father gone daft in his senior years?

Or had she swindled his father? Had she conned him into giving her full operating control—at least temporarily—of his properties? Was her plan to convince Frank to remove him as administrator, thereby giving her sole ownership of all his assets once he died? His teeth clenched in his jaw, and his fingers uncurled only to wrap around the chair arms. Could that be her plan and why she savagely attacked him?

Suddenly, he could not wait until their next meeting. Daughter? Ha! He had a lot to say to his "little sister."

Frank gripped the cane and climbed to his feet. "Come with me, son. I can tell you won't rest easy until you read the documents for yourself."

For once, his dad was right. He certainly needed to see these facts for himself, spelled out clearly and legally in black and white. Then the next time he met River Gallagher; he would be prepared for whatever she brought.

****

Early the next morning, Calder adjusted his tie, straightened his jacket, and frowned at the sign in front of him. One hundred forty-two Edgewater Court. Watercolors. What a perfectly ridiculous name for a property management company. Such a name sounded more like it belonged to an art gallery, and looked like it, too. He studied the soft pastel swirls and letters splashed over the sign and huffed out a disgusted breath. Ridiculous. Nonetheless, and doubting how well the properties were actually being managed, here was where he surely would find River Gallagher.

After a discussion long into the night with his father, and a detailed review of the legal documents, he was ready to straighten out things. Hopefully, this time she would not have the baseball bat handy.

The bell chimed overhead, and a gray-haired, heavy woman at the desk looked up. She eyed him through her thick, dark-framed glasses and gave him a polite, professional smile. "May I help you?"

Calder glanced at the name plate resting on the corner of her tidy desk—Daphne. He stopped in front of her, beaming. "Good morning, ma'am. Is Miss River Gallagher in?"

"You are not in the book as having an appointment," she stated, without glancing at the closed book in front of her.

He took her action to mean she either was not in yet or had no appointments first thing in the morning. "I am Calder Finn. I believe she will want to see me." After yesterday, he sure as heck wanted to see her again.

Daphne wordlessly reached for the phone. "Calder Finn to see you." She replaced the phone a moment later and turned back. "Do you care to have a seat?" She waved toward a small group of chairs along the wall. "She might be a moment."

Nodding, he went to the first chair, searching his memory. Did he know this woman? He did not recall anyone named Daphne, but he might have known her only by a last name, which was so often the case here with kids and adults. Miss Somebody or another. Could she be retired from somewhere he used to go? Coming up blank, he let his eyes travel slowly over the beach-inspired photos along the walls until he heard a door open and heels clunking on the tiled floor. Looking up, he sucked in a breath, his heart fluttering once and stalling as he forgot to breathe.

Was this the same woman who launched an attack yesterday, swinging a bat like Ty Cobb? He could not reconcile the two women. Gone were her jeans. Today, her metallic blue miniskirt revealed miles of lean legs, leading down to thick red heels linked with countless gold studs. Her sequined white blouse sparkled under the fluorescent lights, as did the bangles on her wrists and earrings swinging from her ears. She had enough bling to be seen from the moon.

A faint hint of floral reached out, further assaulting him as she extended her hand. Touching her, he felt the warmth and softness, only secondly noticing each nail was painted with tiny white stars on blue backgrounds. If not for her small mole on the left side of her chin, he'd think he was looking at a twin sister instead.

"Mr. Finn. What a surprise."

He took note that while her tone was cordial, she did not bother with even a false smile. She was professional but not overly friendly. He realized he was still holding her hand. Startled, he gave himself a mental shake and released his grip. "I am here to discuss this matter of liquefying my father's assets. It seems you are currently the person holding those."

She took a step back. "We can talk. But there isn't much to discuss now. Frank's instructions are clear. I assume you already studied his documents?" She arched a cinnamon-colored eyebrow.

"Yes, I did." Did he ever. Thoroughly, late into the night, he combed over the papers with the proverbial fine-toothed comb. "I still would like to speak with you, Miss. Gallagher."

She shrugged.

He could not help but think she doubtlessly thought talking to him now wouldn't hurt if it made him happy. Her arrogance goaded him. Did she feel so confident in her role that she could use him for entertainment? He silently counted backward from ten.

She glanced over toward Daphne. "When is my first scheduled appointment?"

"Nine thirty."

She checked her bling-filled wristwatch and swung back to Calder. "You have fifteen minutes, Mr. Finn. This way." Spinning on her studded heels, she headed back to her office.

She was polite and professional down to a fault. He did catch how she subtly emphasized the word scheduled when asking her receptionist about appointments. So, she was a stickler for timetables? Well, they had that much in common at least. He followed her floral scent down the hall and decided to reserve final judgment until he saw how reasonable—or unreasonable—she could be. After their meeting yesterday, he'd be willing to bet she had an unreasonable streak hiding not so deep under that professional polish.

River entered her office and resumed her chair behind the mahogany desk. She shuffled a stack of papers to one side.

He assumed that meant he interrupted her work. He took a moment to glance around, to better educate himself about the woman he was about to deal with. He firmly believed knowledge was power, and now he needed all the power he could find.

The high-heel shoes were everywhere. That was immediately obvious. Not only the gold-studded ones on her feet, but on her desk as well. Leopard-print, plastic tape dispenser, zebra-striped cell phone charger, and neon-green-dotted pen holder, all shaped like high heels, sat strategically and artfully around her desk. Did she also possess a high-heel-shoe fetish? He wasn't sure what to make of the woman across from him. She was a complete contrast.

Penelope would never be caught dead with such bric-a-brac or the colorful bling. She was more into monochromic design.

"So, Mr. Finn, I assume you have thoughts about your father's properties." River rested her hands on the desktop.

Her words brought him back to the matter at hand. He forced his gaze off her star-studded nails and up to her cinnamon brown eyes. Did she purposely use bling to distract her customers? "Yes, I most certainly do." Down to business—he liked that. He adjusted his tie. "You surely know I am executor of my father's estate. My purpose in coming back to town was to settle affairs."

Her smile slowly spread over her face. "Except you have no legal rights or recourse until Frank Finn is dead," she stated. "Until then, I am trustee of his estate and all his assets."

"Yes, I know that—"

"And I hold power of attorney."

"Yes, of course—"

"And am holder of his living will."

"Miss Gallagher, please!" he blurted, reining in his temper as he fought desperately for composure. She would not get under his skin! He curled his fingers into tight fists at his sides, and he sucked in another breath, silently counting backward from twenty-five.

Her smile faded, and she lifted one eyebrow again, waiting. Her fingernails tapped the desk.

"I am very aware of your control, your power, at the moment, Miss Gallagher. I was hoping in light of my father's current condition, we could reach some sort of mutual conclusion to this matter." One that would allow him to return home quickly. And hopefully never to come back.

She kept her brow lifted and drummed those starry nails in rhythm on the desktop. "What do you have in mind?"

He swept his scrutiny over the room, searching for a clue to her motivation. Taking in the photos of her family and the lighthouse at the end of town, he selected his words. "You obviously have strong ties to this town. I have a life and business of my own to return to. The sooner we can solidify this matter, the better."

"The better for whom?"

"For both of us." He offered her a charming smile. Where he summoned the power to be beguiling was beyond him.

Finally, she rested her chin on her upturned palms, leaning closer. "What are your plans for the properties? They will be considerable once you inherit it all."

Most of the town as he recalled. "My success so far has been property development in Atlanta." He weighed his words carefully. Her cinnamon eyebrow arched again. Drawing a breath, he knew he had her interest. Leaning a little closer, enough to breathe in her perfume, he moved ahead. "Together, we could develop the land. My father owns enough acreage here to put up permanent housing. We could bring commerce, recreation, and industry to this little town."

She withdrew from the desk, her smile fading until it disappeared completely. She rested her palms on the flat surface. "We are not interested in commerce, recreation, or industry, Mr. Finn. This is Sweetwater Harbor, North Carolina, not Atlanta, Georgia."

Realizing he was about to lose her, he back-pedaled swiftly. "I noticed many nice towns along my drive in that offered elegant hotels and fine restaurants. Surely you are not opposed to attractions that will bring in people and places to accommodate them once they are here? Some growth and progress?"

"We have plenty of attractions to bring people here."

"Such as?" Seagulls flapping in the wind? Personally, he couldn't wait to get away. The whole place reminded him of those desolate outposts where wagons hauled by teams of mules dropped off their provisions on the way through. "Nothing is new in this place."

She reared back in her seat, and her eyes flashed as she rested her palms flat on the desk. "That is not true. We have a bookstore. And Raine's bakery. And Watercolors, of course."

He blinked at her list...of three names. "Who is

Raine?"

"My sister. The youngest of our group. She runs a bakery over on Crestview Channel."

"Of course. If it were not for the Gallagher sisters and a bookstore, I'd swear I just left town this morning, not fourteen years ago," he snapped. Immediately, he regretted his impatience.

"Mr. Finn."

Her even tone warned him, as did her brown eyes lighting up. He heaved a heavy breath, hands spread flat on the desk. "All I am saying is we could bring in arts, entertainment—"

"Sweetwater Harbor doesn't have room for more people. We only have a couple of hotels and just a few restaurants. Where do you suggest we would put all these new people?"

"We could develop the land. First, we should do away with the older houses and outdated buildings, we need to construct taller buildings, we could fill in the areas deemed unbuildable until now. Then maybe build condos along Channel Street. And finally, we could make this town a match to any of the other equally-sized ones along the coast."

She shook her head. "We are not interested in what those towns might have done, Mr. Finn. They have overcrowding, traffic jams, pollution, and a host of other problems Sweetwater Harbor does not. And the town leaders wish to keep things that way." Her lips pursed together.

Her tight-lipped expression and narrowed eyes looked like a dare. Town leaders? Of which his father was one. And her parents. Anger gripped him as he saw he had lost the argument. "What town? Sweetwater

Harbor isn't a town. It's a narrow little community of like-minded individuals." And his dad and this River Gallagher were the worst of the lot! They were both determined to keep Sweetwater Harbor locked in the dark ages.

River glanced at her watch. "Mr. Finn, we are not interested in growth and progress in the ways you are suggesting."

He huffed another impatient breath. Counting backward wasn't helping. "Why not? Are you personally resistant to forward thinking?" He glanced at her collection of high-heeled office accessories. "Actually, I am disappointed. I had the impression you were more cosmopolitan. You certainly don't sound like it now though."

Her eyes narrowed into mere cat-slits. "That is the most insulting thing I have heard." Leaning back until she sat ramrod straight, she picked up a file and looked away. "Your fifteen minutes are up, Mr. Finn. Until the situation with Frank changes, I don't believe you and I have anything further to discuss."

Calder blinked, his jaw gaping at what just transpired. He'd tried his best to appease her, kept his cool for the most part, and she dissed him like an unwelcome pest. He pried his fingers from the armrest of the chair and stood.

She flipped through a file, seemingly oblivious to him.

Calder was sure his jaw dropped nearly to the floor; except she gave every indication of not noticing. He slammed it back closed with a hard click that rattled his teeth. He had the sudden urge to snatch the file from her sparkly painted fingertips, toss it across the room, or shred it to confetti, and crawl over her desk to get her undivided attention.

Insulting? Give him a moment, and he would show her what insulting really was! In his life, he could not recall another time when he'd been so rudely dismissed!

He cast her one final look. She continued to study her all-important file, her lowered lashes grazing her cheeks. He swore she was humming to herself, and fresh anger boiled over him.

Hot words died on his tongue as he saw himself out.

Chapter Three

Calder raged out to his car and slammed the door. He'd never been dismissed from a place in his life! Yet, she had the gall to say he offended her! Ha!

He wrapped his fingers around the steering wheel and let out a low hiss. She could insult a mule! Stubborn hellcat was as contrary as one!

Cranking the key until the engine started, he turned it off again. He had nowhere to go. Despite his strong desire, he could not just leave town and return home. Not yet. Not when he still had business here. Not that he couldn't get anywhere with the Gallagher female. But that still left business with his father. After last night, he knew their next meeting would be awkward at best.

Again, he turned the key and revved the engine, looking left and right. He had to get off this block. Anywhere but in front of her ridiculous sign. Opting for left, toward Magnolia Lane, the main drag of town, he headed for the Sound.

A tall, black tower came into view—the south lighthouse of the two that rimmed the town. To the north was Beacon Light and this one to the south was Currituck Light. He stopped his car at the spit of land on the point and sat. He stared at the blue water, the stately structure, the blue sky dotted with clouds, and the boats cruising into the sound.

Ever so briefly he considered if Penelope were here with him. What would her reaction to Sweetwater Harbor be? He smiled, imagining her wrapped in layers of clothing and still complaining. Tops on her list would be a complete lack of entertainment attractions and shopping opportunities, closely followed by the relentless cold and wind. In a word, she would hate this little town. Of course, he wasn't particularly in love with the town either.

Since his return, he'd been fighting off memories, especially those strongest in his dad's house. Now, sitting here, he remembered another time. Just after graduation, he had packed his car, a rusty Chevy Nova with different-colored doors and hood. He said goodbye to his dad and left town. He stopped one time, here at the Currituck Light, to briefly say goodbye to his childhood and the town that was all he had known.

Once he left town, he worked hard to put Sweetwater Harbor behind him. He worked the graveyard shift, delivering pizzas to hungry third-shifters in factories and construction sites and crazy drunks too intoxicated to know whether he brought them pizza or pancakes. But through those modest and horrible beginnings, he earned his education and rightful place as co-owner of Finn-McGee Developers. Their logo of F over M was proudly posted on many banners throughout the city, downtown, and even sprawling into the suburbs. Meeting Brody while finishing his degrees had been a huge benefit for both. Like-minded in their ambitions and plans, they could pass for brothers. Except Brody had not hailed from the tiny dot of Sweetwater Harbor.

Blowing out a breath, he shook his head. Now what

made him think of all that history? Climbing from the car, he stood beside the door, breathing in the scents of salt air and watching the sea gulls wheeling and crying overhead. He smirked; this display was the town's greatest entertainment. And by golly, he hated it.

He yanked at his tie. River Gallagher was just plain impossible. Utterly incredible. Dealing with that contrary, insulting female was as impossible as moving a mountain. Staring at the waves rolling up to the rocks, he frowned. Now what?

Devil of a good question.

First, he needed to check in at the firm and let Brody know what was going on. He thumbed the number for Matt, their right-hand man. "Matt, it's Calder, just checking in. How are things going?"

Matt launched into a monologue so detailed Calder suspected he was reading notes from stacks of files, which would not surprise him. Three people specifically needed desperately to talk to him, and only him. "They have to talk to either you or Brody, so tell them I am out of town, and they have a choice between you two or waiting indefinitely for my return."

"Yes, sir, I'll tell them all just that."

Calder again suspected Matt was taking notes verbatim of his order. "Good. Now, where is Brody?"

"He's in a meeting now, sir. Would you like his voicemail?"

"Yes, that will work." He waited until Brody's recorded voice came across. "Brody, I'm still in Sweetwater Harbor. Matt has instructions. I'm not sure how long I'll be here. I ran into a couple of unexpected complications. Don't worry. Nothing I can't handle. I'll be in touch soon."

He ended the call with a press of his thumb, wishing Brody were here in person. He was so logical; he would know what to do about that spitfire Gallagher female. He pocketed the phone and scratched his chin. He sure had no clue what he should do with whole mess. Unexpected complications…that was a huge understatement.

He might as well return to the house and talk to his father again. Drawing in a deep breath, he shook his head and looked skyward. Maybe he should just go back to Atlanta. He suspected he wouldn't accomplish much here anyway. Indecision gnawed during the short drive back to Finn Summit. He climbed the stairs, knocked, and then let himself in. Voices drifted from the living room. Rounding the corner, he recognized Muriel Gallagher seated on the sofa. Great, another Gallagher female to contend with. How on earth did old man Gallagher handle all those women in his life? He had what…four of them? A wife and three daughters. The man must have the constitution of a rock.

"Well, hello there, Calder. It's good to see you back home," she greeted.

Her smile was warm and genuine. She had the same cinnamon brown eyes as River. Calder nodded in response to her greeting. Had her manners matched River's at one time too? Try as he might, he couldn't picture grandmotherly Mrs. Gallagher hot-tempered like River. "Thank you, Mrs. Gallagher. To what do we owe this visit?"

She waved toward Frank. "I was just bringing your dad some sugar for his coffee." She inclined her head to the small bag on the counter.

Calder's face fell, his shoulders slumping. "Dad, I

would have brought that for you. No need to bother your neighbors. No disrespect, Mrs. Gallagher," he added quickly.

Frank shook his head and tapped his cane. "Too much trouble finding you larking about. I know where Muriel is."

"I have a cell phone. You could have called." Why did he suddenly feel sixteen again?

"Calder," Muriel broke in. "Did you know your name means stream? It's a Celtic name."

"No." He had not. That explained why he and River where at opposite ends of their discussion. What happened when a stream met a river? Honestly, he did not know that answer either. Or was it a matter of a river meeting a stream? Either way, a smooth blending did not seem to be the possibility here. He caught the glance Muriel sent his father and wisely decided not to share his latest encounter with her daughter.

Suddenly Muriel climbed to her feet. "Well, I should go. Cordell is no doubt wondering what happened to me, and he'll be wanting something to eat soon. Calder, it is so good to see you back." She patted his arm.

Her friendly pat had a way of making him feel like such an adolescent…eight…or ten years old.

"Now, Frank," she continued, "don't let your excitement over Calder's return overtax you now."

Calder took a step back. Overtax? He'd never considered that his dad, who was clearly frail and dying soon, would get too excited by his arrival. Had he been too forceful in their discussions? He barely felt Muriel's slender hand as she briefly touched his shoulder before she let herself out. "Hey, Dad, are you okay?" he asked.

"Can I get you something? Coffee? Another blanket?" Concern crowded his mind as he sought for something to do.

"How did your visit go with River?"

Calder bit back a groan, sinking into the spot Muriel just vacated. Floral perfume wafted into the air. "Dad, I really don't want to talk about her right now, okay?" He might be feeling guilty with his dad, but not enough so to open a discussion about that she-cat he adored like a daughter. Disgust filled him.

Frank grinned, looking out over the water. "Then tell me of your life in Atlanta. And afterward, you can go pick up our dinner in town. Who are your friends? Did you marry? Am I a grandpa?"

How was he supposed to answer? Doubtlessly, his dad would be pleased with his business success. That he would appreciate his close friendship with Brody, and the life he had carved out for himself. At least he hoped so. Except how would he explain the reasons why he was marrying Penelope Jordan? Would he ever understand?

****

River locked the door of Watercolors, exhaling a tired sigh. Today had been a long day, and a productive one, and from a business point of view, successful. Daphne departed a couple of hours ago, leaving her to lock up alone. That was fine with her. After today, she needed some solace.

Looking out at the lights blinking off the dark waters of the harbor, she remembered she'd not eaten since eleven o'clock. The time was now well past seven thirty. Almost eight, she confirmed, checking her watch. Too late to start something at home. Maybe she'd just swing by the restaurant and grab a takeout. She'd treat herself to something she normally didn't eat. After her early morning visitor, she deserved it.

After an exhausting day, she was worth it. Fifteen minutes later, she was heading home with her dinner-to-go from Newport Diner, counting down the minutes until she could slide into a warm, relaxing bath. As she passed Finn's Summit, she remembered needing to discuss one quick matter with Frank. Her dinner would keep for the ten minutes she would require to run in. After parking the car, she climbed the stairs, rapped twice, and let herself in. What a shame she had not thought to get Frank a little something from the restaurant. Well, she could always run back if he wanted anything. She'd make the offer.

"Hello, Frank, how are you doing?" She found him standing at the window, staring out over the water. Peering past him, she saw the darkness of the bay and the revolving flash of Beacon Light reflecting off the water. He leaned heavily on his cane, and worry pricked her heart. Pain twisted inside her chest. Losing him would hurt so much! "Can I get you anything?" She came to a stop alongside him and touched his shoulder gently. "Have you had dinner yet?"

He smiled and patted her arm. "Fine, my girl, I'm fine. Just thinking is all."

"That's good. Um, where's Calder?" She glanced around, nerves vibrating as she realized she was also in his house as well.

"The boy went out to fetch our dinners at Newport Diner. Should be along shortly."

Newport? They must have just missed passing each other.

Frank turned around, a smile playing on his thin lips. "He won't tell me about how your meeting went this morning. Would you care to?"

She sighed and pushed her hair off her shoulders. "Frank," she began, picking her words carefully. "You and I are very similar."

Frank nodded.

"And Calder seems to be a very different sort of person. Maybe it's because of the big city influence. I don't know."

"But?"

She winced. "But he's different. He's difficult."

Again, Frank nodded. He moved back to his chair, cane tapping the floor. "Boy always had his own ideas about things, even as a youngster." He leveled River with a hard stare. "But then again, so did you as I recall."

Again, River sighed. That was the problem with growing up with the same people all your life. They remembered your younger years. "Regardless, however true that might not be, Calder and I are certainly not similar. He's…"

Words failed her as she recalled the flight of the butterflies in her tummy when he first arrived for his appointment and how insulting he turned once it became clear they were on different pages on everything. The man had a way of shaking her up like a blended dessert, leaving her feeling both hot and cool at the same time. Like one of those chocolate desserts with heated fudgy centers. You think you're getting one thing until you bite down and find the hot surprise in the middle. The flight of butterflies soon gave way to the angry gathering of bumblebees. She gave a mirthless laugh, not sure how to answer.

"He's Calder," Frank supplied.

At the telltale smile on his gaunt face, she cringed.

"I'm back. Did I hear my name?"

River jerked around her head, heat flushing her face as she took in the man leaning against the doorjamb, arms folded over his chest. Two white sacks emblazed with Newport's logo rested on the counter beside him. How long had he been standing there, listening? "You're back." She rose, hating that she just stated the obvious and feeling like a deer trapped in the headlights of an oncoming car.

****

To her credit, she blushed. The fact surprised Calder. From the moment he returned and spotted her ridiculously small econo-car in the parking spot, he felt the dread uncoiling in his gut. Every time he climbed these steps inside, the climb became heavier and harder. And then he opened the door, heard their voices, and her perfume immediately reached him. The heady scent filled his already tangled mind, and he wasn't sure whether to enter or leave.

Pride made him enter. Curiosity made him stay.

No way could he have missed the tender way she looked at his dad with that concern in those cinnamon eyes. Just like he could never miss how they flickered to other emotions when she spotted him. Surprise at first, then embarrassment, then a readiness of something else—something he could not identify. She had more moods than he had neck ties.

"Well, I must go. My own dinner is waiting." She stood, gaze still on Calder's. "Frank, I'll be back later. Tomorrow maybe. So, we can talk." Her hand rested lightly on Frank's shoulder.

The point was clear. She wanted to talk to his dad without him around. No prizes guessing what that conversation would be about. Irritation rankled him until he caught the look his dad tossed him. Was it just him or did his dad look overtaxed? Overtired? Mrs. Gallagher's warming echoed in his ears. "Look, uh, River, maybe we got off on the wrong foot." He pulled away from the doorjamb. "May I walk you outside?"

She nodded and returned once more to Frank. "Take care. I'll be back." Turning back to Calder, the honey warm look she gave his dad was gone.

"Fine. Are you ready?"

The cool appraisal look was only matched by the crispness in her tone. Marveling at the sharp contrasts, he extended a hand, waiting for her to precede him, knowing she would not touch him softly like she did his father. The thought both saddened and puzzled him at the same time.

River moved down the steps and stopped, leaning against her car. "So?" Brushing her hair behind her, she regarded him, her lips tight and eyes hooded. She tossed her bag inside the car and crossed her arms over her chest.

Inhaling the salt air, he shifted his feet, hands going into his pockets. The sea breeze lifted and played with her hair. Overhead, seagulls cried. "Like I said upstairs, I believe we got off to a bad start," he began slowly. "We are two mature, realistic people." He waited for her slow nod. "I think we can discuss these matters in a better fashion." He lifted a shoulder, giving her a hopeful grin.

"Do you always dress like that?" she asked, hands

falling to her hips, head tilted.

Startled, he reached for his tie. "Like what?"

"Like you just walked off Wall Street."

Somehow, she made the comparison sound like a bad thing. Normally, he would have taken the words as a compliment, but not from her. He adjusted the buttons on his overcoat. "This attire suits how I live. I find it comfortable." This statement coming from a woman who could single-handedly light up a room with her sparkles. He eyed the glittering crystals racing up and down the black sleeves of her sweater. The glitter matched the crystals he knew were on her white blouse peeking from underneath. Tempted to ask her the same question, he held his tongue by firmly pushing it into his cheek.

"You're right." She gave him a small smile. She turned back to the car and reached inside for her case.

She held the briefcase before her like a weapon. Calder kept a respectful distance, not putting it past her to fling the case at him.

Instead, she withdrew a card and handed it over. "Call Daphne, and make an appointment this time. We can try again." Releasing the card into his palm, she opened the car door and slid in. She slipped on a pair of sunglasses and skillfully backed out the tiny car, around his larger rental, and onto the road. With a parting wave, she was gone, puttering into the fading sunset.

Calder stood in the center of the road, watching her taillights slowly fade. He wasn't sure what he expected when he asked to start over, but somehow, this wasn't it. Despite her fairly easy acceptance of his suggestion, and his palm cupped the card as proof she had agreed with him, he still had the sense she somehow played him.

What was she really up to?

****

River considered stopping by her parents but decided against it. Right now, she was hungry and needed some distance between herself and Calder Finn. The man had a way of affecting her in ways she could not begin to name. One moment she felt funny in her tummy, and the next she wanted to slug him with Storm's bat. Distance was a friend right now. Her parents and her business with Frank would both have to wait.

Reaching her own house a few streets over, she parked and circumvented the front door and headed for the sandy back yard. Surrounded by sea oats and salt grass blowing in the wind and wheeling sea gulls, she pulled close her sweater and faced the chilly air blowing past the lighthouse.

Beacon Light Island stood like a rocky sentinel only half a mile away. If she left the curtains open in her bedroom at night, she could watch the revolving beam flash over her walls. When the moon shone through the skylight over her bed, she sometimes imagined she was a fairy princess. What a silly fantasy, left over from her childhood in which she dreamed of princesses and princes and castles in the sand.

She pushed aside both her hair and the whimsical thoughts and stared at the waves rolling in, highlighted by the lighthouse beacon. Now she had no time for girlish fantasies. Watching as the water broke over the gray rocks of the island, she grimaced. The man rolled into town smug as sin—and sexy as sin to boot—and within minutes had her seeing red. If she wanted to keep herself under control when she was around him, she needed to start now…before their next meeting.

She had the feeling he and Frank were not on the best of terms. Even in just the few moments she spent with both men in the room, she couldn't deny the increased anxiety once Calder made his presence known. She gritted her teeth. If he ever hurt that sweet old man, he'd get far worse than a slugging with a baseball bat. He'd wish he'd never returned to Sweetwater Harbor.

For that matter, how long did he plan on staying? She recalled the day Frank and her parents telling her he had left. He was eighteen, and she was fourteen. He'd just graduated high school; but she was getting ready to start. He'd raced out of town in his beat-up car like the devil himself was after him. He had made a few initial visits home for holidays and such, but they became shorter and farther apart until they stopped altogether.

Frank volunteered one day that even the phone calls had stopped.

River assumed no contact meant Calder Finn was happy with his own life he built someplace else. So, why was he bothering to hang around now? Surely, he didn't expect Frank to up and die for his convenience, did he?

Well, maybe she'd get some answers when he returned to Watercolors for another appointment. This time, she would hold on to her patience, regardless of what was said or what happened.

A boat's horn sounded as it chugged into the harbor, turning for the marina south of her house. She waved at the captain and headed back to her car for her dinner. By now, it would be cold, but she could reheat it. Inside, she heard her dogs barking. After dinner, maybe she would take them for a run on the beach and then soak in a warm bath. Something herbal. Then she could slip on her favorite silk pajamas, brew a cup of her favorite tea, and slip into bed with the dogs and a plate of snickerdoodle cookies. The moon would rise and filter through the skylight. She'd watch comedy shows on late night.

Tonight, she wanted to pamper herself—and forget all about the odd, conflicting ways Calder Finn could affect her thinking.

****

River rolled over and slapped her alarm clock into silent submission, shoving one of the dogs out of the way. She raked a hand through her tangled hair and considered going back to sleep. Half an hour? What was the harm?

She had not slept well, with images of Calder Finn popping into her mind with all the finesse of runaway cattle. Now, tired, she glared at the expectant dog faces, ready for another romp on the sand. Not this early.

She could call Daphne to check about any immediate appointments. If not, she could sleep in and head into Watercolors later. She reached for the phone, but before she could get her hand around the body, it rang, startling her and the nearest dog. "Hello?" She stretched out an arm to soothe the dog.

"River, this is Horace Hardy. I hate to bother you so early on a Monday, but I have a favor to ask."

Despite her concern, River smiled. Horace was not one to normally ask for help. She heard the frustration in his voice. "What can I do for you, Mr. Hardy?"

"Those nephews of mine took out the boat sometime during the night. They somehow disabled the poor thing."

Scenes painted themselves in her mind as he paused to blow out a disgusted breath. Horace's sister and brother-in-law were both stationed overseas in the army. He and his wife were temporarily raising the boys, ages nine and twelve. In the meantime, the two nephews were known for raising trouble in the town. River's mom once pointed out she suspected they were simply acting out their worries with both parents gone serving in the military. "Are the kids all right, Mr. Hardy?"

"Oh yeah, they're fine. Someone brought them back earlier. But I need a ride out to get my boat and hope she starts."

River's fuzzy brain connected the dots finally, all thoughts of extra sleep drifting away. "You want me to drive you out to *Wasting a Weigh*?" She'd always liked the name Horace Hardy called his boat.

"Yes, if you have time."

She could almost hear his slow nod over the line. "Of course." She'd make the time. "Meet me at the marina, at the *Wind Quest*, in half an hour, okay?"

Letting out the dogs for a fast break, she headed for the shower. She'd have to grab a bite of toast on the run while she checked in with Daphne. Five minutes later, she started the car and dialed the office as she backed out of the driveway. "Any appointments this morning? For the first few hours? Something has come up, and I need to go out in the *Wind Quest*."

"Mr. Finn called and booked a ten o'clock time," Daphne said.

Mr. Finn? River paused. Why was Daphne's tone dry and disapproving? And why would Frank call and book—? *Calder*. She almost rear-ended the car in front of her that stopped for a pedestrian. That was fast, she thought, regarding how quickly he made a new appointment. "Okay, so what's his number? I'll call and reschedule. Anyone else?"

Scribbling down his cell phone number, she found herself curious how flexible Mr. Calder Finn could be about his appointment. He seemed so unyielding about everything else; surely he'd be put out about adjusting any appointments. Traffic resumed moving again as she dialed his cell.

He picked up on the third ring.

"Calder Finn."

At his baritone voice, she instantly noticed the sudden flopping in her tummy. She swallowed and told herself the motion was hunger, not satisfied at the single piece of toast. "Hi, it's River. I hear you have an appointment this morning."

"Yes."

"Would you be willing to meet me at the marina instead? In one hour. Do you remember where it is?"

****

"Yes," Calder replied. Now what? He eased his car to the side of the road and threw it into Park. He knew in his gut this call would upset him. What made him think a simple meeting with River could go as planned?

Staring at the phone in his hand, he shook his head. The woman was impossible. If she wore a mood ring, it would be forever amber for all her changes. She was like her namesake—a river, flowing along, always changing and never the same.

The marina! A flash of irritation spiked through him. What the devil could she possibly want to discuss at the marina? Of course, he remembered where it was. How insulting. How irresponsible. He felt the creases of a frown. Did she always run her business this sloppy? "I remember where it is."

Without further preamble, she ended the call. Calder stared at the phone cradled in his hand and blinked a couple of times. Had she just hung up on him? *Really?* The woman was impossible! He clenched his teeth as his fingers tightened around the phone.

He better wrap up his business with her soon, or he would be tempted to wring her pretty little neck!

****

River puttered into the marina's parking lot and spotted Horace Hardy where he waited. Anxiety clearly lined his weathered features, yet a smile crossed his face when he spotted her.

"Those kids—" He strode over to meet her, wringing his hands.

"Don't worry, Mr. Hardy. I'm glad they're safe." She took his arm and headed for her boat. "Let's go find *Wasting a Weigh*, okay?"

Climbing aboard her eighteen-foot cabin cruiser, River prepped and plotted their course for where the kids were picked up earlier. "She could not have drifted too far away." She started the engine. With a loud rumble, the *Wind Quest* came to life. Like a seasoned pro, she eased the boat from the dock and into the open harbor.

The sea air felt good on her face. This was a good day for boating. Lately, she did not take out the *Wind Quest* often enough. The boat had been a family gift for her twenty-fifth birthday, and in the three years she'd owned the fine vessel, she found herself busier and busier with less time for her favorite pastime. Where was her life heading?

"There she is!" Horace Hardy pointed.

His words drew back River's wandering thoughts. She steered over to the smaller boat bobbing on the waves.

Horace scrambled across to board his pride and joy vessel.

"Well, she still floats," she stated, glad Horace had found his boat.

He turned the engine, and it roared to life. "And she starts." Horace wore a huge grin. "Bet those kids just couldn't find the on switch again," he muttered.

"She ought to run then. I'll follow you back to port," River said. "Wave if you run into any problems." Watching the older gentleman happily take the helm of his beloved boat, she settled back in the captain's chair. Finding *Wasting a Weigh* had not taken long, so the return trip should be short. Hopefully, she would not keep Calder Finn waiting too long. Now that the crisis was solved, and she had time to think about it, she did feel sort of bad for calling him like she had. But a check of her watch showed the time was past ten now, and meeting here was the only way to salvage their appointment.

Not to mention, this situation afforded her the chance to take out the *Wind Quest* for a soothing spin before another ordeal with Calder. The man could upset her thinking on so many levels.

Chapter Four

Calder stood by River's car, where it sat parked at the marina. He glanced around, fists tight, and ground his teeth. The woman was not only sloppy in her business dealings, she was now tardy—in addition to everything else. He consulted his watch and frowned. The time was now one hour and ten minutes past the time she phoned him with new instructions. Then she doesn't even keep those. Impossible! He dragged a hand over his jaw to keep from clenching another fist.

Seething, he looked at her car again. Empty. Abandoned where she left it, no doubt to go off lollygagging on some sparkly errand that caught her eye. He touched a palm to the cold hood and snarled. "Hell of a way to treat scheduled appointments." He flagged down a fisherman smelling of fish and grease, and he pointed to River's car. "River Gallagher? Have you seen her lately?"

The old salt smiled. "Little River? Sure, she's out about there somewhere." He jabbed a thumb over his shoulder at the open water of the bay.

Calder watched as new wrinkles added themselves to the weathered ones permanently etched on the old man's tanned face and swallowed his disbelief. "You mean she's out on a boat?"

The fisherman chuckled. "A boat or the back of a dolphin, boy. But I'm betting she's on her boat." He slapped Calder on the shoulder. "Don't worry, boy, she'll be along presently." With another laugh, he ambled off.

Calder had forgotten the dialect of the people native to Sweetwater Harbor. No one in Atlanta dared to address him as "boy." This place had a way of making him feel fifteen again. And he hated it.

Just as he loathed the ever-present cold wind, even in the height of summer. And he disliked the constant stench of fish and salt and the cries of the sea birds.

Turning his gaze back to the water, he spotted two boats approaching, one following the other. The first was a small fishing boat, and the second a handsome cabin cruiser. He bit back a groan as he spotted "Little" River Gallagher at the helm, smiling and the wind blowing her hair into tangles. The sight stirred something in his gut.

Wordlessly, feeling stiff as the painted buoys he stood next to, he watched her expertly slide the vessel into its berth and lithely lash the mooring lines. A joyful smile competed with the rosy glow in her cheeks. The sea breeze pulled her blonde locks, lifting them like the manes of the wild mares that galloped on the sandy shores.

In a word, he was thunderstruck. At many things. At her apparent non concern about their appointment as she dawdled up late, and he was awestruck at her radiant happiness. The happy glow shining on her face told him she was clearly in her element. This new facet of hers left him clueless on how to approach her. Much like approaching wild mares, he could not storm up and demand explanations for her lack of business etiquette.

He forced himself to look over at the old man and

watched in silence as he secured his boat.

Finished, he gave River a wave. "Thanks for the help, River. Hope I didn't keep you from anything important."

She shook her head, casting a look over at Calder. "No problem, Mr. Hardy. You take care now, and say hello to the missus for me."

Calder watched as she blew out a big breath and gave one final tug on the boat rope. Was it his imagination or was she looking a tad nervous? Bright color highlighted her cheeks, giving her a healthy radiance. He sucked in a steadying breath of his own as she walked up and gave him a big smile.

"Hello. You found the marina, I see."

Patience, he reminded himself, pressing his tongue into his cheek as he matched her pasted-on smile. "Yes," he murmured. They had to remain neutral or they would never make it through this meeting, and he would never get to leave town.

He watched as she pulled wind-blown tangles away from her face. He shivered from the cold air rolling in from the ocean, and an idea struck. "Let's go for coffee," he suggested. "It's quite chilly out here," he added at the instant question in her eyes. And the location served as neutral ground.

She gave a slow nod. "Bobbers is just over there." She pointed to the diner that sat on the corner of Long Point and Lake Side Boulevard. She fished her keys out of her jacket pocket. "I'll meet you. Watch out for the drawbridge."

This time, if they were in a restaurant, she couldn't storm off in a huff or chase him away. He had been half afraid she'd do something crazy out at the marina, like what he didn't know. He suspected anything was possible with her, though. But now he had her trapped at the tiny diner table. She'd fixed her tangled locks, and her lips shone as glossy as her outfits as they slowly pulled into an alerted *O*. Did he look so furious? Doubtful. But she did look like he was about to bite her. Except she would very likely bite him back. Wordlessly, he slid into the seat across from her.

She shrugged out of her jacket.

For the moment, he decided to keep on his overcoat. Tension built, becoming palatable as the dessert bar across from them.

"Coffee?" A server approached, carafe in hand.

"Please." River flashed two fingers. "Two of them."

The server wordlessly poured the coffee, her eyes narrowing at Calder and her eyebrows reaching up into her hairline.

As the server slopped coffee onto the table, he studied River's tight jaw. He felt like she'd just slapped him. Once both cups were full, she hastened away with just her strong floral perfume left lingering in the air.

He wiped up the coffee spills and wondered what happened that this woman distrusted him. He shrugged it off, took a sip of coffee, and immediately set it down. The brew was incredibly hot, scalding his tongue, burning his throat on the way down, and shooting off flares once it landed in his stomach. Glancing over at River, he saw she cradled the mug between her hands but had not yet taken a drink. Well, now he knew why. The lethal stuff could also probably peel paint once it cooled—if it did not solidify into a molten mass of sludge first. Heaven only knew what it was doing to the lining of his stomach now.

"So, here we are," she spoke quietly, with only the barest twitch of her lips.

"Yes."

"The coffee gets better once it has a chance to cool."

Ignoring the growing movement of amusement in her moist lips, he stoutly slugged another rip down, just barely resisting shouting flames of profanities.

"What exactly do you hope to accomplish during your stay here, Mr. Finn?" she asked.

He set aside his cup, having had enough of the flaming acid for now. Resting his hands on the scratched tabletop, he selected his words carefully. "Sweetwater Harbor is in a prime location and perfectly launched to support new growth. Lots of the old buildings here could be razed and make way for such great improvements to this town."

She frowned, then took a long swallow of her coffee.

For a moment, he was lost in her throat bobbing as the liquid slid down.

"The coffee is good. Your words were terrible. Don't you realize this wonderful old diner belongs to your father? Surely, this couldn't be one of those outdated buildings you're referring to?"

Of course it was, but he suspected she'd only be angry if he confirmed it. Instead, he glanced around at the old paint, scuffed floor, and ripped upholstery. As he walked inside, he'd noticed one corner of the building's foundation sagged into the sidewalk. It truly looked to be just a question of time until the whole building collapsed. Wonderful old diner? Well, she had the old part right. Clearly, they differed on the definition of wonderful. Equally clear was the fact she liked this derelict building.

"You have such great plans for the town," she said, setting her cup down yet keeping it close. "But as I have said before, the people here have no interest in nor can they afford the country-club housing you're suggesting. The country-club people and wealthy businesspeople who you want to attract won't want to come here. And besides, have you considered the residents who live and work in this town? In those old, outdated places you are referring to?"

"Of course."

"How they will be affected by all the progress?"

"They would not be expected to leave." Heaven knew some of them could not be moved out of here with blasting dynamite. His father and her parents were content to stay forever. Was she included in that group too? Was her plan to live and die here, never having seen the wonders of the rest of the state? The region? The country? The world? Did she have any idea of what was waiting outside this map-dot of a town?

Looking at her tangled hair and glossy lips, he had to wonder if she'd ever leave the tiny seaside village. Why were her roots so deeply planted here?

The diner's doors opened, and a chime toned.

He turned to see a middle-aged couple and a little boy enter, and then he turned back to River. Strangely, he found himself fascinated by that glossy frown as she heaved another sigh, a sad sound, and turned her gaze out the window to the boats bobbing in the harbor. What was her motivation? "What are your plans?" he blurted before he was fully aware he spoke the question.

"Excuse me?" She pulled her gaze off the harbor activities to meet his eyes.

"Plans," he repeated, fumbling. He could feel his eyes rounded in surprise at his own boldness. Should he risk another drink of that toxic brew to buy some time? "What are your plans?" He opted to see this course through instead.

She cracked a brief, sad smile.

Her expression slammed into his chest like the cold wind howling, grabbing his full attention. He forgot the coffee and rested his hands on the tabletop. His fingers traced scars carved into the surface.

"Long term or short term?" she asked.

The breathy whisper of her voice nearly undid him. So did the sad look in her eyes. "Both."

She leveled her elbows on the table. "I want to honor your father's trust in me."

The words, so softly and sincerely spoken, sucker-punched his gut. Her earnest expression assured him how seriously she took that trust. He could not help the prick of admiration for her integrity. Whatever his other thoughts about her might be, she was determined to do right by his dad. That was far more than he could say for himself.

Okay, hard to argue with that. More people moved around the diner, two sets of customers leaving and another set entering. People laughed, the bell rang, dishes clanged, and through it all, his attention never strayed off River.

"What about you?" she asked.

A sigh escaped him. He might as well mention it. "Get married."

She cracked a slight grin. "Someone particular or just anyone who happens to be handy?"

Her tone, somewhere between lightly teasing and a droll mocking, nettled him. "Someone particular. I am engaged to be married next month."

"Really?" She blinked. "Does your intended know about this?"

He planted his palms on the table, like he'd seen her do, and narrowed his gaze. "Of course she does. As it so happens, she is merrily making plans back in Atlanta right now." Why was he suddenly uncomfortable discussing his engagement with River Gallagher?

She arched an eyebrow, taking another sip of coffee. "What's her name?"

"Penelope Jordon."

"So, why are you here instead of back there"—she gave a flick of her wrist—"helping her plan your wedding?"

He shook his head. Even if he were back home, which he would greatly prefer, he would not be doing much planning. "Penelope is seeing to all the details." All she needed was his checkbook. Or her daddy's.

He met River's curious stare, fighting the urge to fidget. What was she thinking? He was almost tempted to try another sip of the vile concoction they called coffee here, just to break the emotions between them. He worked to draw a full breath. Now, he wished he had removed his coat. He reached for the sleeve, as her words stopped him.

"You don't love her," River said suddenly. "And she doesn't love you."

Her tone was soft, almost sympathetic. A bolt of

defensiveness shot through him like hot lightning. "Our relationship is not like you're making it sound," he snapped. "You know nothing of Penelope and me or our relationship."

"A marriage of convenience," she stated as she gave a soft sigh. She rested her elbows on the table and shook her head.

He opened his mouth to object, then closed it. Of course love existed between Penelope and him? Love and passion and heavy breathing and emotions.

Right?

Different emotions, not like the ones passing between him and River right now.

Penelope's daddy owned most of downtown Atlanta. Between what Calder already owned in the other parts of town and the sprawling burbs, they would make a great combination, speaking from a real estate point of view.

So, how much did real love have to play into this relationship? They had enough between them.

Didn't they?

Meeting River's patiently waiting gaze, he looked away. Blast this woman, but she was more correct than he cared to admit, now that he was forced to think about it. But how had she known? Had his doubts shown that clearly on his face? Surely not. He felt so transparent with her.

"Are you telling me you would never marry a man if it were just mutually beneficial between you? Is that what you are implying?" he challenged her, bringing his palms back to the tabletop.

She shook her head, moving tangled hair out of the way. "No, I would only marry for true love and nothing less."

He envied her confident answer. Yet, it explained why this tumultuous woman was still single. However, his curiosity won out. "Okay, and what do you consider nothing less than true love?" Was there even such a thing?

She smiled.

Her smile was the first real smile he'd seen from her. Almost dreamy, it slammed into his chest with all the tenderness of a bulldozer. He counted the seconds until he could force a shallow breath back into his lungs. One…two…three…four…five… Would she ever answer him?

"That's hard to put into words. It's more something two people will feel when destiny speaks, and they are the right two."

He could have almost laughed, if he had been able to breathe properly. "Then you think it's destiny that makes two people fall in love?"

"No. I think destiny brings them together. They fall in love because they are meant to."

Ah, crystal clear, considering it was coming from her. "Well, that is an interesting point of view, I suppose." He brushed off any crumbs that might be on the table or stuck in the scarred ridges. "However, my arrangement with Miss Jordon is my business and none of yours, so kindly keep your opinions to yourself."

"You asked."

Yes, he had. Blasted woman messed with his mind. "We really need to discuss the matter that brought us here. When I inherit my father's estate, I will develop this town. Now, with my life and business, and soon to be my wife, in Atlanta, I will need someone here to help." He watched that eyebrow slowly rise and paused as his breath hitched. Who knew an eyebrow arching in anticipation could be so sexy? "Do you think we could work together to grow Sweetwater Harbor?"

She took another sip of coffee. "You mean collaborate?"

"Yes, I suppose so. You seem to have some skills at property management. With my directions, could you competently manage and develop the town for me as you have for my father? To my expectations and specifications?"

Her brows dropped, and her hands slapped the table in unison as she rose in her chair, her eyes rounded. "That is most insulting, Mr. Finn! Some skills? You haven't the foggiest notion of what I have done for your father. Perhaps you ought to ask him!"

"Are you angry?" He forced his tone to remain mild, aware of the other patrons turning their direction at her outburst. Flames of anger practically shot out of her brown eyes as she grabbed up her purse and jacket. He barely suppressed the urge to duck.

"No, Mr. Finn, I am offended. When I am angry, you will most certainly know. I believe our business here is done."

Calder watched her storm across the tiled floor, her feet stomping.

She yanked the door and let it slam behind her.

The bell clanged as it smacked the glass and he winced, hoping it didn't shatter. He glanced around, not sure what to say and decided not to say anything at all. Hopefully, the locals were accustomed to River's bursts of anger. The collected number of suspicious glances made him wonder what they thought and who was to blame for their conversation.

He laid down a few bills, slowly rose, and let out a long breath. So much for a quiet discussion by the bay. He stepped outside, looked out over the water, and wondered if he should try engaging her again. What could be worse—her storming out of the room after shouting in his face or her causing his heart to throb irregularly when he looked at her?

****

After stomping her way through the parking lot, River pushed her little car as fast as it would go the three blocks to Watercolors. For once, she wished she could just drive, far away from the insults of Calder Finn. Parking all too soon at work, she clomped through the side door.

Daphne inhaled sharply. "Mercy, River, darling, what happened?" She set down her mug and placed a hand over her heart. "You look like—"

"Calder Finn. That's what!" She poured a cup of water, thrust it into the microwave to heat, and yanked a packet of cocoa powder from the shelf. "We met at the marina, ended up going to Bobbers, and he is the most insulting excuse of a man I have ever known." The microwave beeped and she jerked out her mug, tipped in the cocoa and stirred so hard the powder spilled over.

"Here, let me, dear." Daphne eased her aside, as she took the spoon, and stirred.

"He's engaged to be married."

Daphne sniffed. "Pity the poor girl."

"Oh, it's a marriage of convenience."

"He told you so?" Daphne handed over the mug.

"He didn't deny it." She took a sip. "Sounds like it's a real estate venture."

Daphne inhaled again, then took her mug and River's elbow in her other hand, propelling her to the front. "Either way, it's none of your affair, my dear. Hopefully, you'll never have to meet the future Mrs. Calder Finn."

River bit back a grin. With Daphne's accent, Calder's name came out sounding more like a part of a fish. "Let's hope so." She gave a nod and took a drink of cocoa. She wasn't sure she could handle another emotional meeting with him. Calder Finn had a way of bringing out the worse in her temper like no man ever had before.

****

Calder stepped out into the cold wind blowing off the ocean. The cool air felt good and whisked away the heat in his cheeks. He jabbed his hands in his pockets, glanced around, and wondered what to do. No way was he having another meeting with that little hellcat. Once he inherited his due, she would just have to deal with whatever his plans were. If she could not collaborate, that was her problem.

He wished Brody were here. Brody would have some good words of advice. Staring at the light tower in the distance, he considered his few options. He had no friends here. His dad was glad to see him but still barely spoke much. Maybe he should just return home. Today, while the hour was still early. With any luck, he could be back in Atlanta by dinnertime. He could pick up Penelope if she was not busy with some social function or another, and maybe, they could take in a play or something after dinner.

Now, that sounded more like a plan.

Returning to his car, he reached for his phone,

ready to call Brody and Penelope with the news of his return. He slowed for a vehicle creeping along the road. As his fingers impatiently tapped the steering wheel, he considered what they might be up to. Brody would be working late, and probably eating Chinese at his desk. Penelope most likely had plans with her girlfriends and wedding ideas to buzz about.

The slow-moving car pulled into a parking space. He heaved a sigh of relief. Maybe the better option was to wait and surprise them once he arrived. First, he'd go back to his dad's, pack, say his final goodbye, and contact the airline about a return flight. He would be looking at almost a two-and-a-half-hour drive to the airport and the time to return the rental car and check-in to contend with. Hopefully, he could book a flight in the next four hours.

Driving through the main street of town, he glanced around, making mental notes on the ages of the buildings his dad owned. The holdings included the physical businesses and the rental homes, the monetary assets, and the undeveloped land outside of town. Like the open land over on that peninsula in Currituck Sound. A lot could be done with all that pristine beach. Those beachfront zones just begged for high-rise hotels and maybe even a casino. He'd have to check the zoning laws to see about any restrictions. Once he was in the air, he could start plotting and planning in earnest.

That nasty little diner could be razed and easily replaced with something more upscale. The employees would have the option to be retained. That should keep River happy. As far as the marina, he had no clue yet what, if anything, could be done to upgrade that eyesore. He might investigate dredging the harbor to allow access for larger ships.

Excitement coursed through him. There was so much to plan. This is what he loved about property management!

He pulled onto Finn's Summit and studied the landscape. These houses were the oldest ones in the town. They were also among the largest. Should he keep the old house? He could find other uses if he chose—a B&B maybe—or he could simply sell it to be free of the memories. Perhaps he could turn it into the company headquarters for this location. Ideals spun in his head like the wheels of his car.

Stopping in his dad's driveway, he parked, his hands on the wheel as he stared at the old house that once was his home. Yes, this was the best way. He'd contact the airline and then say goodbye. He did not want to cause his dad any further upset or stress by either his staying on or his leaving. A quiet exit would be best. Plan made, he climbed from the car and left his overcoat in the passenger seat. He rapped once at the front door, and it swung open with a dry squeak.

"That's odd." While not locked, he at least expected it to be latched. Perhaps the Gallagher's were visiting and had not closed it all the way. "Hello?" Hearing nothing, he entered the front room, still fully expecting voices to reach out to him.

Only silence greeted him. Eerie silence. Unnatural silence.

"Dad? It's Calder. Where are you?" He entered the living room, expecting his dad to be in his usual chair or perhaps by the window overlooking the bay. Instead, he stopped, breath escaping from him as he struggled to take in the scene.

The room was a mess—furniture knocked over, lamps broken, glass shattered, cords ripped from the walls.

Staggering into the room, he struggled to process the sight, his heart racing. "Dad?" His voice squeaked. Then he saw the tip of the cane and his dad's gray slipper. "Dad!" Scrambling, he fell, sliding across the wooden floor to his dad's side. He shoved aside the chair. "Dad, talk to me! It's Calder, your son!"

Fear choked him as he felt for a pulse. Finding none, he felt again, heart hammering. "Dad!" he sobbed, pulling his dad's body into his arms. "Who did this?" Who in this miserable little town would ever have a need to do this? What could they have been looking for?

"Dad." He cradled the still form to his chest. He touched his fingers to the cold blood, congealed on his dad's temple. Gaunt before, he looked ghostly now in death. "Oh, Dad, I'm sorry I wasn't here to protect you." Like River had done that first day he arrived. Like River would have done had she been here when whoever broke in. Like he should have done, instead of planning his exit. "Oh, Dad." Tears, hot and salty, fell, dropping to wet his dad's shirtfront as he tightened his fingers over the thin shoulders. "Forgive me."

Sirens blaring nearby broke into his grief, startling him. Sirens now? Had someone called the police? Well, they were a bit too late, weren't they? Gently easing from under his dad's still form, irritation goaded him to his feet. The sirens stopped in front of the house, and resentment flared through him.

"Halt! Don't move!" an officer barked as he roared

into the room. He shoved a gun in Calder's face. Three other officers immediately followed.

At the sight of the weapon, he stood straighter and his eyes widened. He stabbed a finger toward his chest. "I live here. This is my dad, and he's dead." He got the word out past the lump forming in his throat. *Dead*. His end really happened. Just not like Calder had expected. He wasn't supposed to die brutally like this. He was supposed to slip softly away in his sleep. "Look around you, man."

"Freeze!" The officer reached for Calder's shoulder.

Stunned, Calder felt himself spun around and his hands yanked behind him. "Wait a second! What are you doing?"

The second officer knelt at Frank's head, checking for a pulse. He gave his partner a negative wag of his head while the third and fourth officers searched the adjacent rooms. They sounded like a pair of bull elephants.

"Any weapons on you, sir?"

"Weapons?" He jerked backward and shook his head. "No, of course not. Are you mad?" He shivered as the officer started a pat down. "My father has just been killed, and the house ransacked. What are you doing?"

The officer slapped a pair of metal cuffs over his wrist. "Arresting you for the murder of Frank Finn."

Calder's brain locked on those few words. He felt the cold cuffs biting into his flesh, and the officer's rough hands. He turned his head and stared at his dad. He was so pale and still. Was this really happening?

Chapter Five

River took a seat on the barstool and propped her elbows on the counter, watching as her little sister patiently spread the frosting. "What's this one going to be, Raine?" At this stage, the dessert could take on any of the imaginative shapes and sizes Raine was known for creating. Right now, River needed a shot of her sister's reflective calm—and something seriously sweet.

Raine blew out a breath, lifting her dark bangs as she studied the tiered pieces. "Eventually, it will morph into a birthday cake. At least I hope so."

River grinned. "I have faith in you. It'll be okay." She picked up a dainty little petit four from a nearby tray and nibbled it.

Raine slapped her hand, grinning. "Not for you, River Faith," she scolded.

River shrugged, chewing noisily and smacking her lips in absolute contentment. "Too late, Raine Erika." River laughed and Raine joined her, then River sobered. "Ahh, too bad Stormie isn't here."

"How is Storm? Have you heard?" Raine returned to adjusting the tiers, adding a decorative piece and more frosting, blending the sections together.

Again, River shrugged, reaching for another cake. "Out chasing the wind, as usual."

Raine frowned and pushed the plate out of River's reach. "Those are not for you. Did you stop in here just to eat me out of business?"

Sweet Obsessions was Raine's pride and joy, a bakery where she experimented not only with pies, tarts, and cookies, but she created masterpiece cakes that bordered on displays of art. Though she opened only two years ago, she built a fine reputation as a master baker and confectionary designer.

"No, I needed to—" How could she explain how she was feeling right now? "Since when do I need an excuse to stop by and see my baby sister?" she challenged instead.

"Never." Raine lifted her shoulder in a shrug before returning her attention to the cake, her brows knit. "But it's not like you to be so melancholy. Who has been bugging you? I could punch him for you."

River's eyes rounded on her sister. "What makes you so positive it's a who?" she asked. "Or a man even. Maybe it's a what?"

Again, she lifted her shoulder, her eyes flickering only briefly over to River. "Maybe. But my money's on a who. A male who. You are infamous for your distrust and general loathing of men." She hesitated, the slightest twinkle in her eye. "But I bet one has finally broken through your armor-plated skin. That handsome son of Mr. Finn perhaps?"

River's mouth flew open and slammed shut, sending jars of pain radiating through her face.

"Mom told me," Raine said. "She said you and he were as combustible as kerosene and matches."

Flattering. *Not*. River searched the walls of Sweet Obsessions, taking in the framed prints of some of her sister's more imaginative decorations alongside antique cookie cutters and cake molds. Then, at a total loss for how to respond, she was saved when her cell phone rang. "Oh, it's her. Hey, Mom, Raine and I were just talking about you. Were your ears ringing by chance?"

"I am so glad I reached you, River. Have you heard the news?"

"No, what's going on?" All thoughts of teasing vanished at her mom's serious tone. Horror slowly stiffened her face. She turned to her sister.

Raine stopped her work, her hand holding the spreading knife suddenly caught in midair.

"Okay, I'm on my way. Bye." Turning to Raine, she slid off the barstool. "Sorry, kid, but I have to go."

Raine caught her arm. "Frank?"

River nodded, her eyes already misting. Her throat tightened in a painful vise. "He's dead."

"I'm sorry—"

"And Calder's been arrested for his murder."

"Here, take this, wherever you're off to." Raine set aside the blade, picked up a chocolate petit four, and pressed it into her sister's palm.

Looking at the sweet cake, River couldn't stop her tears from spilling. "Thanks, kiddo. I love you, too."

She left the store, the chocolaty goodness filling her mouth. Her initial thought was to go to her parents' house. They could console each other until she was required to step up in some official capacity. Except she did not feel like doing anything official. Right now, she wanted to mourn the passing of a dear friend. She climbed into her car.

But, as her mom explained, his passing not been the peaceful eventual end everyone had been anticipating. Instead, he died from a brutal attack, at the hands of an assailant, in a home that now resembled a battlefield.

Heat burned through her as she drove out of town. If only she could have been there... She slapped the steering wheel, sniffed, and wiped away the tears with her sleeve. She hadn't been and it was too late now. She reached Finn's Summit, slowing at the sight of the familiar weathered road sign. Suddenly, she slammed on the brakes, bringing her intelligent car to a shuddering halt. One block from her parents' house, she had a better plan.

Unless she was mistaken, she had some hard choices to be made right now.

Turning the car, she headed south, toward the drawbridge and out of town. Fishing her cell phone out of her pocket, she called her mom's number. "Mom, I just wanted to tell you where I am headed."

****

Calder spun in another tight circle, cursing his luck, and anything he happened to think of. Lately, he'd had nothing but bad luck. And so far, it seemed to be getting worse by the hour. His father was murdered, the house ransacked, and the killer and crook were running free. Meanwhile, he was stuck here, cooling his heels behind the black bars and against the gray, cinder block walls. And his arresting officers were quite content to ignore his calls for help. He had not even been given his one free phone call to summon assistance.

If that was not absolutely infuriating and depressing. Once he did get a call out to Brody, he could just imagine his shock and horror.

Tugging at his tie, he dropped onto the lumpy and incredibly uncomfortable mattress. Who broke into the house? Well, broke into was a bit of a stretch since the door probably had not been locked in the first place. Who entered with such malicious intent? What were they searching for? Because clearly a search, however hastily, had been conducted. He remembered that much from the scattered pictures in his mind of the last few hours.

Who had anything to gain by Frank's death? Other than him, of course. That probably, more than anything, explained why he was locked in here like an animal while the real killer was out there somewhere. Talk about your circumstantial evidence.

Sheer frustration pushed him on his feet again, prowling the short confines of the cell. The only redeeming grace, if any was to be found, was he had the cell to himself. The constant moaning, singing, laughing, and farting of his neighbors in nearby cells were enough to make him want to climb the walls or chew the bars. If he had to share cell space, he'd probably do something incredibly rash. Perhaps his jailors sensed that and kept him alone as a result. Or perhaps he'd just gotten lucky for once—if that could be considered lucky. He snorted.

Gripping the bars, curling his fingers around the cold steel, he gave them a mighty shake. They did not bend. Why was he stuck in here? He was innocent! He gritted his teeth and tugged again, to no avail.

"Finn!" a guard barked.

"Yes." Mentally shaken from his anxious tugging, Calder dropped his hands.

The guard stopped before his cell. "Let's go."

"Go where?" Oh mercy, if they were taking him farther into the dank bowels of this miserable place, he'd fight them. "I'm innocent. My father's been murdered. Why do you insist on—" He instinctively backed away and raised his hands.

The guard inserted the key, turning the cell door with a hollow click. "You can explain it all to your lawyer and at your trial. Right now, your bail's been posted, so you're free to leave." He hesitated. "Unless you want to stay."

Stay? "No!" Bail? Who would know about him being stuck here and then care enough to post his bail? Surely, Brody had not somehow heard the news? He would not have had time to arrive yet. Maybe he wired the funds. The Gallaghers next door, perhaps? That made sense. They could not help but see the police arrive, with blue lights flashing and sirens blaring, and him being hauled off in the humiliating handcuffs.

Thoughts buzzing around his cluttered mind, he followed the guard through twin sets of more steel bars, each one clanking loudly behind him. At the last one, he signed for his personal possessions in a brown envelope—watch, wallet, credit cards, keys, phone. They were all accounted for.

"Don't plan to leave the area anytime soon, Mr. Finn," the officer behind the worn desk stated dryly.

"Excuse me?" Calder stopped midpoint in strapping on his watch. Leaving, and immediately, was foremost on his mind.

"The area of Sweetwater Harbor. Not until the police have had time to finish their investigation. Do you have a lawyer? If not, one can be provided for you."

He'd heard the appointed lawyer bit during his arrest. "Of course, I don't have one here. I have a company lawyer back home in Georgia."

The officer shrugged. "Better see if you can book him on a flight in. You might want him here."

Calder closed his eyes and clamped his teeth tight, inhaling deeply. The whole nightmare was getting worse and worse. Forget the extra cost of having the lawyer fly in for this mess. That was just one small piece.

"Exit's that way."

He did not have to be told twice. Whoever was waiting on the other side, whoever posted his bail, just might get a kiss. Wouldn't Brody have an attack? Eager to escape, he nearly sprinted for the sign labeled *Exit*. He swung the door and looked around, searching for any familiar faces.

He slammed to a stop, inhaled sharply, his heart trip-hammering. His stomach plummeted to his toes, and his thoughts kicked into a frenzied wild beating. His mouth went dry, and he wished for a drink of cold water. Or something a whole lot stronger. There stood his rescuer…River Gallagher.

"Nice to see you too," she said dryly. "If you'd rather not come along—"

"No, no!" he interjected, reaching for the door and yanking it open. "We can go."

He followed her out to her ridiculous little car and stood, looking doubtfully at it.

"You'll fit," she assured him, climbing in.

"You frequently drive men around who are my size?" He pulled on the passenger's door, hoping it did not break off.

"If you want to leave here, you'll fit." She turned over the engine. "And I have a tall brother."

That was right. He remembered now. One of the

sisters had a twin brother. The middle one, wasn't it? So, where was he now?

The ride along Highway Twelve was passed in silence. He fit in the car, barely. But, at least, he was not in the jail. Despite the cool air, he lowered the window a fraction, just to take in the fresh, salty air. He stole a few glances over at River, noticing her tight grip on the wheel and her frequent blinking. He initially thought it had been the lighting back at the jail, but now, he knew the truth. She had been crying. And she was trying hard not to cry again. At least not in front of him.

Crying for his dad? Probably. Had she been to the house yet? Seen what he had? He was torn between shock and anger now, too numb with both to feel like crying. But he suspected the grief would come later.

The drawbridge, red warning lights, and red taillights from cars loomed ahead, and she slowed, bringing the car to a stop third in line at the drawbridge. She sat, her gaze fixed straight ahead, her jaw quivering, and watching how brave she was trying to be killed him.

"Where are we headed?" Calder finally asked. If they ever got across the blasted bridge, he could…. What? His mashed-up mind could not even think of a plan. But staying in this mini car with River much longer, with her floral scent surrounding him, and her soft sighs assaulting him, was worse than staying in the jail cell. She looked at him, long enough for him to see the mist on her eyelashes. That sucker punch slammed into him, taking his breath away.

"Home, I guess," she replied.

"Great, I can start cleaning up the house and—"

"No, my home," she interjected. "You can't go back to Frank's right now."

He snapped his head to look at her, his jaw agape. He forced his mouth shut long enough to ask, "And why not?"

"Because it's a police crime scene. They have it taped off."

Stunned, he stared, speechless as pictures of yellow caution tape rolled through his mind. Why had he not thought of that? Because his mind had been preoccupied lately. Suddenly, his chest labored to draw a breath, and he lowered the window another inch. He wished he had his overcoat, but he'd left it in the front seat of his rental, which was no doubt taped off with police barrier tape.

He reached up to massage the back of his neck where a knot of tension knitted together. So, he was forbidden from leaving town, could not return to his dad's house, was without his things, and without a place to go. Was he even allowed to go inside and see if anything was missing? Probably not. What a predicament. Except she said they were going to her home. He cast her another look, ready for that sucker punch this time. "Why your place?"

She bristled, then she drew in a long breath, her gaze locked on the passing masthead, and her knuckles white on the wheel. "Because you need some place to stay. You will probably not find too many friends in town right now, so I am offering you my home until Frank's is open again."

She had a point, a few of them, and a generous heart—larger than he had given her credit for. Since he's had some time to think about it, maybe he had been a little harsh about how his words came out when they were in the diner. Playing them back now, she did have a right to be insulted. No wonder she couldn't look at him. He'd been a jerk, and she responded with kindness.

But honestly, he had not meant to sound that way. His words just came out poorly. The boat passed, the warning lights stopped clanking, and the bridge started down. He expelled a deep breath. "Look, River, about what I said when we were at the diner, I'm sorry."

She gave him that sad look again, her eyes moist.

He had the oddest desire to reach across and wipe her tears. He raked a hand through his hair, something he seldom did. "What I meant to say then was more, I was hoping we could work together professionally, and I wanted to put my faith in you as much as my father had. So, I'm sorry it came out all wrong."

She nodded, stepping on the gas as the cars in front moved ahead. "Forgiven."

He blinked. That was easy. Somehow, he'd expected to have to work harder or longer to earn her forgiveness. Once more, she surprised him. They crossed the bridge and were back in town. He sighed, looking around at his town now, for all general purposes. Somehow, he thought it would come with a feeling of great power or something akin to that. Instead, he just felt hollow, empty, and cold. He raised the window a fraction.

"You'll have to start making some hard decisions soon," River pointed out as they puttered along Magnolia Lane.

He gave a dry laugh. "I don't even have a change of clothes or a toothbrush. How can I make a decision on anything?" Suddenly, he felt overwhelmed, unprepared for what he thought he was ready for. The last few hours changed everything.

She lifted her shoulder in a shrug. "I can help with the clothes and toothbrush. But the decisions are pretty much yours."

He knew what she meant. With his dad gone, the rules of their agreement changed. Suddenly, his opinion of River Gallagher shifted incredibly. "Why?" he asked, believing she would understand he meant posting the bail.

Blinking rapidly, she shrugged again. "Because I know you didn't kill him."

He felt vindicated to hear the positive conviction in her voice, but he had to ask, "How can you be so sure?"

She cut him another sad look. "Because, for starters, you were with me when it happened."

Good point. But he wanted to press on, to understand her better. "But how do you know I didn't hire him killed? To be timed while I was conveniently out of the house?" If he considered it, no doubt the police and others would, too.

Her sad expression slowly lifted into a real smile. "Enough rumors are already going around about what you planned on doing to Sweetwater Harbor once you inherit it. It's easy to see no one around here would like you enough to do something like that. Not even for the money."

Another good point. She had a knack for finding them. Which also meant plenty of people were willing to point the finger of blame at him. His only alibi was the time he spent with River until they parted at the diner.

They cruised past Finn's Summit, coming to Surfsong Circle, a crescent-shaped bit of sandy road topping the town before Highway Twelve headed farther north toward the barrier islands and Virginia.

"You live up here?" Her house was only a few blocks from her parents and his dad's house. If he tried hard enough, he probably would see the yellow tape flapping in the ocean breeze. Not that he wanted to.

"Last house on the street." She nodded. "I suppose the police said for you not to plan on leaving?"

He nodded. "How did you know that?" Again, that shrug.

"By now even the police would know you are the only one with anything to gain from Frank's death. Of course, you're a suspect, most likely their number one or only one. So naturally, they can't let you just skip out of town." She paused as she pulled into the driveway. "Actually, a lot of people around here would benefit if they had killed you instead."

A sobering thought. Ironically, she had the most to gain by his premature death. Even more ironic, he was the only one in a town of dozens of people with a motive and the only one the town residents would prefer to see dead instead of Frank. Now, how could that be any more depressing and upsetting?

Opening the door, he heard excited barking to indicate she had a dog. Sounded like more than just one. At least they were contained out back.

"Don't you like dogs?" She reached behind the seat for her case.

This time, he shrugged. "I was bit once, which left a bad impression." He was dating a woman in Atlanta and her slobbering beast of a something tried to swallow his hand when he offered it a treat. Since then, with that really his only experience with dogs, other than seeing one or two in passing on a leash, he avoided them as a species.

"Well, if they will be a problem, you could always try getting a room at the inn back in town," she pointed out slowly. "But don't be surprised if they suddenly don't have any spaces open."

She had another fine point. His options were few. If they were confined to the back, he'd simply avoid the back. Easy enough solution. He wasn't dating River; he was not obligated to make friends with her dogs.

She gave a small laugh, reaching out to punch his arm. "Come on, Calder, they're small dogs."

Hearing her call him by name with the familiar contact galvanized him, spurring him with that gentle-as-a-bulldozer sucker punch. He climbed from the car and followed her up the stairs to the entry level. Like all houses built on the beach, hers was elevated on stilts for protection from the hurricanes. And like most houses in Sweetwater Harbor, she didn't lock the door. She turned the knob, throwing the big door open and a clean citrusy scent reached out to welcome Calder.

"Mama's home, babies!" she called, dropping to one knee.

The excited barking from out back intensified, and soon he heard the scrambling of toenails on the wooden floor. Two little scruffy dogs tore around the corner, mouths open and tongues lolling. He stood rooted at the spot.

Sweeping the dogs into her arms, she laughed, lifting her chin just out of licking range as she scrubbed both enthusiastically around their ears.

Standing with hands in his pocket, Calder was spellbound at the sight. Sheer delight for both River and the dogs. Terriers of some sort, to judge by the short, scruffy hair. But River commanded his attention. She was delighted with their reception, their tails wagging, and their happy paws getting closer as she giggled and stroked their backs.

"Okay, guys, that's enough," she said at last, brushing them off as she rose to her feet. Still smiling, she regarded Calder. "They, uh, get happy when I come home."

Understatement, and she was clearly just as happy to see them. Her eyes sparkled like the earrings and bangles and outfits she wore. She practically glowed. What would it be like for her to glow with joy like that for some man? To greet a man she loved with such wild abandon like these hairy creatures just greeted her? She would never marry but for real love, he remembered her bold comment. A bolt of amazement knifed through him.

Now where had those insane thoughts come from? Startled by his errant mind, he swiftly shook his head. "Yes, dogs do that I guess." He felt at a total loss. "What are their names?" He eyed the panting pair, still staring adoringly at their mama.

"This is Pepper, and she's a Scottish terrier." She petted the slightly larger black dog. "And the white Westie here is Salty." She grinned. "Salt and Pepper."

"Clever." He got it. Good thing she didn't have a red dog, one of those Irish Setters or whatever. She'd probably call that one Ketchup.

Hands still in his pockets, he glanced around. Beyond the hall they were in, he could see a large, open floor plan that flowed seamlessly from room to room. Her décor favored Southwestern design. Colors of cool turquoise, coral, and sage seemed to be the dominant theme from what he could see. Windows rimmed the seaside view, and he spotted fluffy clouds in the distance over the harbor. Beyond that was the towering presence of the Beacon Lighthouse out on its island. Swinging his gaze back to her, he drew in a shaky breath. "So, now what?"

Chapter Six

River stood at the stove, stirring their supper. She thought about take-out, considering everything going on right now but decided instead for the soothing peace cooking offered her. Thai curry chicken, one of her favorite dishes, would hopefully go a long way toward easing the butterflies in her tummy. And some of the tension hanging so heavy around the house.

In the next room over, Calder paced the floor, talking on his cell phone and his feet beating a rapid tattoo on the wood floor. He made at least a couple of calls already, one to his partner back in Atlanta, and now he talked to the funeral home who had Frank's body, deciding on arrangements. He alternated between raking a hand through his hair and flinging an arm through the air. She supposed they all had to be awkward, difficult phone calls to make. She glanced once more toward him and lifted the lid off the wok, releasing the spicy aroma.

Seeing his hair thoroughly mussed from repeated rakings, she had to admit Calder Finn grew into a handsome man. Right now, he was also an exasperated one. His hair stood in ruffled spikes and his silly tie was loosened. She liked the rough-edged look, even if she suspected great frustration caused it. No longer polished, he looked more approachable. Dare she even think hot?

A short time ago, she'd made a call of her own, to her mother, who was surprised but delighted when she gave her request. Hopefully, Calder would be half as happy. She wondered what made the man happy. Quite a lot from what she had seen so far. But then she was used to men who were never satisfied. Did Calder qualify as one of these, too?

Giving the contents a stir, she replaced the lid, trapping the aromas again, and wished she could trap her memories and feelings as easily.

"Yes, that sounds fine," Calder said, his voice carrying from the other room. "I'll be in touch tomorrow. Two o' clock it is."

Looking up, River saw him approaching, pocketing his phone as he came. His expression was somewhere between somber and weary. Poor guy had to be exhausted, mentally if not physically. Bracing herself, she waited.

"Hi." He halted a few feet away.

The uncertainty in his eyes was palatable, like smoke hanging in a room. She felt as unsure as he looked but decided casual was a good approach. "Hi. All caught up?" She nodded toward the pocket holding his phone.

"For now. I'll undoubtedly have more calls to make, and other calls to repeat later. And this is just the beginning."

Poor Calder looked so shattered, she wondered if he'd make it through dinner. "Are you hungry?" She was famished. When was the last time she ate? Raine's chocolate petit four. That seemed like days ago instead of hours.

He nodded. "Yes."

She smiled, lifting the lid. "Great. Grab a plate. Dinner's done." Spicy scents escaped, swirling around the steam. Curry, paprika, cinnamon, and others.

Calder smiled tentatively and took the plate she offered.

River filled her own plate, adding liberal amounts of rice as the bed before pouring on the meat and sauce. Grabbing a glass of water, she headed for the small table at the window overlooking the harbor.

The pair of dogs followed, quietly settling a few feet away on matching plush beds.

Duplicating her actions, Calder followed, settling across from her. Until now, she'd never noticed how small her nook table was.

"Quite a view." He picked up a fork.

"Peaceful." She nodded as she took a bite and chewed.

He took his own mouthful and immediately froze. His eyes popped wide, and he snatched his glass of water.

"Too hot?"

Gulping down a few, extra swallows, he nodded, "Did my tongue just curl like a corkscrew?"

"Sorry. Must be the chili peppers."

Setting aside the glass, he picked up the fork. "A little hot." He grinned. "It took me by surprise. But it's good." He took another taste, a hand resting near the water glass. "You know, I've been looking at your Southwest décor and now the Thai cooking. Both seem so out of place from this...seaside village. Yet, you carry them both off with ease and grace like someone who lives in a more diverse city."

His words were a rare compliment, and she smiled.

Was it possible he just raised his opinion of her a notch? She took another bite. "So, what are your plans for tomorrow, if I may ask?"

"Nothing too serious. My options are rather limited." He grinned and glanced down at the counter, taking a moment to brush off any debris. "Contact the police and a few other places. Meet at the funeral home at two tomorrow, and I still need to make more calls." He lifted his gaze to meet hers. "Why?"

"I just had an idea or two."

"Which are?"

She could not miss the involuntary wince he made before his question. Just what did he think she came up with? A knock sounded.

The little dogs alerted, barked once, and scrambled for the door, their tails wagging energetically.

She wondered what he had been thinking but let it go for now. "That's probably my mom." River rose from her chair.

Sure enough, Muriel Gallagher strolled into the room, carrying two brown bags and flanked by the happy terriers. Setting down the sacks, she reached into her pocket for two treats, which she passed to the dogs.

Grabbing their bones, they retreated to their beds along the wall. Crunching sounds soon filled the space.

"Calder, hello, dear," Muriel greeted. "I hope you know you have both my and Cordell's most sincere sympathies."

"That's nice, Mrs. Gallagher, thank you." He rose.

He stood, with his shoulders bent like the weight on them was almost too much. River poked her nose into one of the brown sacks and then handed it over to Calder, a ghost of a smile on her lips. "Here, see if these are adequate."

****

"Adequate?" Calder peered in, stunned by the layers of clothes lay neatly folded inside. He lifted an eyebrow at the pile of jeans, shirts, sweaters, plus a pair of sneakers on the bottom.

"Those are some of our son's things he leaves here." Muriel moved forward to pat his cheek.

He suddenly felt like he was ten, though he was beginning to see it was just her way.

"Winter is about your size. He leaves a few bits to wear whenever he gets breaks and can come home for a visit. In the meantime, I'm sure he would not mind us loaning them out."

"Breaks?"

"Winter is in the army. Currently, he's serving overseas. He's Storm's twin brother."

"Stormie leaves a few things behind at the house, too." River's lips twitched. "For when she's home between emergencies. Things like her favorite baseball bat."

He pointedly ignored River's not-so-subtle reminder of the bat between them. "They'll be just fine, Mrs. Gallagher. Thank you."

She beamed. "Cordell picked up some men's toiletries." She nodded at the other sack. "He insisted on going, saying he knew what men needed."

Glancing in the smaller bag, Calder was relieved to see a brand-new toothbrush among the items.

"Well, I don't want to interrupt your dinner, you two, so I'll be on my way. Calder, dear, if you need anything, just let Cordell or me know, okay?"

"You've already done plenty, Mrs. Gallagher. I

appreciate the loan and goody bag. I am indebted to you all, River included." His tone sobered. "You're probably the only people in town who accept me right now."

Muriel's radiant smile faded. "Have you spoken to the funeral home yet?"

He blew out a heavy breath, his chest tightening. The pain of the subject surprised him. "Yes. I'll see about finalizing the plans tomorrow. I understand Dad wanted to be cremated with a memorial service on the beach."

Muriel nodded, tears brimming in her eyes. "Yes, that's what he told us, too. He kept Lola's ashes, so they could be released together into the water."

His lips thinned. "That ought to be interesting. As if sending the ashes of both my parents into the waters of the bay won't be hard enough, we'll be holding a memorial service in a town where I'm hated, and everyone loved my parents." He cracked a flat smile. "Just great."

****

"So, you ready for a road trip?" River asked the next morning.

She strolled into the room Calder had occupied for the last hour, on the phone again. He eyed the terriers at her feet, then swung his gaze upward as he closed the phone. They'd shared breakfast, before going their separate ways to shower, and she said nothing about taking a drive. "Road trip?" He wondered if he had missed something. With River, hard to say.

She nodded. "I said last night I had an idea or two."

Yes, she had, but he was fairly certain the words *road trip* was not included in their conversation. "Trip to where?" Out of town? She knew about his police enforced limitations.

"Around."

Ambiguous. Oh, what the heck, why not? "Sure." He climbed to his feet. He automatically reached to adjust his tie, stopping when he realized he wore faded jeans hugging his hips and a thermal T-shirt that stretched over his chest.

She smiled, taking in his new look. Winter's clothes suited him. "You'd rate at least a seven now. Maybe an eight."

"Excuse me?"

"Eight. Storm likes to rate men on a scale from one to ten. You know, like men tend to rate women sometimes. She figures doing so evens out things."

He did know about the rating scale, though he did not rate anyone based on their beauty. Sounds like this sister, Storm, was a genuine liberal and a real fireball. So, he was a seven or eight? Flattering, he supposed, but what was wrong that he missed being a ten? "Storm would give me an eight, or you rate me an eight?" He met her amused grin. This might be a fun game.

She lifted a shoulder like she tended to do.

"Either of us I guess. Maybe. Or just a seven. Are you ready?" Spinning, she headed for the door.

Snatching up his sweater, he followed, feeling lighter inside than he had all morning.

They idled east, then turning south into town. Taking in the scattered houses, raised on matchstick legs that gave way to clapboard businesses, Calder could not suppress a frown. Sweetwater Harbor was simply a chunk of sandy soil, rimmed by water, that NC 12 happened to cut through, bisecting the town. For some reason, beyond his comprehension, people like his folks, the Gallaghers, and other like-minded individuals carved trails they called roads with pretty sounding names, put up houses and businesses, and gave the whole place a name.

Then they stayed until they died, utterly content, and never once caring about what was beyond the lighthouse and the drawbridge.

The area seemed like the make-believe town of Bedford Falls from the classic movie *It's a Wonderful Life* he watched at Christmas time. Or maybe more like the alter ego of the town, Pottersville, instead, in all its gloomy and depressing limitations. Watching the buildings pass by in a steady blur of color, he brooded and decided it felt more like Pottersville.

Suddenly, River stopped the car on Driftwood Lane and turned. "Are you always like this?"

"Like what?"

"Like you are about to meet with an undertaker."

His frown deepened until he could feel the creases. "Actually, I am." But he also got her point. She did have a knack for finding them. "But, no, I am not always this way." Mostly just since his return here. He faintly recalled a pleasant day on the golf course with friends after a fantastic week, just before the fateful call that sent his world plunging into dark depths. Would he ever reclaim that blissful life that seemed so far away?

She rested her hands on the wheel, letting out a long breath. "Okay, poor analogy, sorry. But tell me this, is it Sweetwater Harbor you hate so much?"

"I don't hate this place." At least, he didn't think so. "I just don't see what you and Dad and all the others see in it." He braced himself, half expecting her anger now that he insulted her beloved town. Like her namesake, the river would overflow, raging and taking him along in the flood of temper.

Instead, she nodded, then reached for his shoulder. "I can help you with that, if you'll let me," she whispered.

Touching him, electricity shot through, from him to her. Her hand stayed until he thought the blazing heat would burn his skin.

Then, licking her lips, she pulled away, exiting the car. "This way."

Stunned, still spinning from her eyes, so large and soft and tender, and the sizzle of her hand on him, he swallowed and followed her down the street. Shoving his hands into his pockets, he trailed her into Tattinger's General Store.

The place was old, the worn wooden boards creaking under their feet, and the shelves were filled with everything from canned goods to shampoo to a modest collection of clothes. One wall housed a butcher counter, and a pharmacy counter lined the back, with bottles of pills covering the far wall. The business seemed to be the place to get just about anything. The whole place smelled of polish on old wood and jerky and faintly of old perfume.

"Hello, Mr. Tattinger," River hailed the gray-haired old man behind the counter, busy counting something in a small box. His gray apron was embroidered with *Tattinger's* across the chest in bright red.

"River, hello, dear. Who is your friend?" He extended a hand.

"Mr. Tattinger, this is Calder Finn, Frank's son."

He dropped his hand before Calder could accept it, his easy smile fading. "Finn, huh? Well, sorry to hear about your dad, boy." The man ran his gaze up and down Calder, his eyes narrowing. "He was a good man, and the town is worse for the loss."

"Thank you for that." Calder shifted uneasily and returned his hand to his pocket.

"Any ideas of who might have done that deed?" Tattinger looked back to River for an answer, having dismissed Calder.

"No, not yet." She shook her head.

Just then a young boy, of perhaps twelve or thirteen, came through the back door, carrying a box almost too heavy for his size. "Dad, I got those—" Seeing customers, he stopped, his comment dropping off.

"Hey, Teddy, how you doing?" River smiled at the boy. "Calder, this is Teddy, Theodore's son."

Calder offered the boy a grin. "Hi."

Teddy slid his load on the counter, turning back to River. "I'm joining the Air Force when I get older. Mama said I could."

"That's great, Teddy." She swung her gaze back to Theodore.

"He'll be just like his old man," Theodore Tattinger Senior predicted. "That was where I met Frank Finn, and he was the one who convinced me to retire the missus here to Sweetwater Harbor once I left the Force." He turned his gaze over to Calder, waiting.

"I never knew that." In truth, Calder just knew the Tattingers were another family who had always been a part of the town. He could not help but notice the proud smile Theodore Sr. gave young Teddy. He failed to remember his dad ever looking at him so fondly.

"Your dad also rented us this store for a good price. Been fair to us all these years. And River here has been a fine trustee for Frank."

He was getting it now. "You think I'll be a bad landlord, is that right?"

The old man shrugged. "When the ship sinks, the rats are nowhere to be found."

And what did that mean?

River touched his arm. "We have to go now, Mr. Tattinger, we just stopped in to say hello." Giving his sleeve a tug, she moved him back toward the front door.

"What was the point in that?" he demanded once they were in the street.

"The point in what?"

"Going in there. You didn't buy anything."

"So I did not. Guess I forgot." Striking off again, she moved across the street to the hardware store.

Puzzled, and more than a little upset, he followed. This time, he was more prepared for the expression of sympathy, then followed by the look of distrust.

"Right fine man, Frank was," Paul Barlow, the proprietor of the hardware store, said. "Good friend and a man who always had time for his friends. His loss is a hard blow to the community. He was honest with all his business dealings with us."

"A man you could depend on," Barlow's wife, Andrea, chimed in. "A man who cared for the people and the town."

"A good neighbor who was always fair in his dealings and treated everyone fair and alike," Joseph Wickmore, the proprietor of the Golden Anchor Inn, said.

"He always put people before profits," Chip Miller praised. He ran the little ramshackle building that housed the post office, among other sundries.

"Surely heaven has gained a sweet soul with the addition of Frank Finn," chimed in Abigail Hughes, who was collecting her mail at Chip's.

"A more honest and fair man you won't find," stated Kelly Westmoreland, from the Dry Dock Restaurant. "He was always fair with us."

They left Westmoreland's place, and River checked her watch. "How about a quick lunch? Before your two o' clock meeting?"

Hadn't they just left a restaurant? Did she plan to drag him off to another one? He wasn't sure he could handle one more person telling him how great his dad was. He dragged a hand through his hair, stood in the wind, and eyed her. "Okay, fine, whatever. But tell me this, what's your little plan?"

"Plan? I don't know what you mean." She slipped into her car, turning it on and waiting.

"I think you do." He folded himself into the small space. "You're dragging me into all these places just so I can hear how great my dad was."

"Don't you think your dad was great?"

He gave a frustrated moan, raking his hair again. "Of course I do. That's not the point here. Why do you feel I need everyone in this town to tell me about it?" She shot him a sweet smile, probably as innocent as she could manage. He didn't buy that.

"Maybe it's more than just what you're hearing them say. Bobbers sound okay? Or Newport Diner sound better this time? Or we could try What If?"

He blinked at the last one. "What If? What is that?"

"Ah, someplace new you don't know about. It's a sports bar and restaurant down on Long Pointe." Smiling, she turned the car toward the south end of town.

Realizing she wouldn't elaborate on her cryptic comment, he remained silent on the five-minute drive to What If? What a name that seemed so out of place with many of the nautical-themed businesses in town. And a sports bar? Really? Since when?

They parked and entered the new, freshly painted building. One wall was covered in windows, overlooking the harbor. Naturally. Another was dominated by wide-screen television sets playing various sport programs. The open kitchen commandeered another wall, and the last wall was flanked by a dance floor. The place seemed to have something for everyone. He had to check, did his father own this property too? If so, could it turn a profit in this backward village?

Arching an inviting brow, he pulled out a chair for River, then sat himself. "Dine here often?" He picked up a small menu. A quick perusal showed they offered normal burgers and basket-type fare, as well as beer on tap and select wines.

"Not very often. Occasionally when I feel like a burger and fries. Their fish and chips are superb."

He replaced the menu, not feeling very hungry. After this was the trip to the funeral home to finalize plans. His chest was tight, and he felt a headache coming on. Food had no appeal right now.

A young server with a curly brown ponytail and wearing a short red apron reading, *What If?* came over, handing out glasses of water. "What will it be?"

"Fish and chips," River stated, "and a glass of white wine."

Calder arched a brow.

"My limit," she assured him.

"Same for me, please."

Before their orders arrived, musicians filed on stage and tuned their instruments. Guitars, bass guitar, drums, and violin all blended into a sweet harmony.

Wasn't it sort of early for the music to start? Or maybe they were just rehearsing.

"Do you dance, Calder?"

"I haven't in a while." Truthfully, he could not recall the last time he had. Somewhere surely. Atlanta had a lively night life. At some point, he must have taken time to enjoy it.

She lifted a cinnamon brow. "Not even with your intended, Penelope?"

"We've never danced, no." Not at a club or any of the dozens of society events she hauled him off to. They drank cocktails or wine and hobnobbed with the "right people." Then they left.

The wine arrived, and River took a slow sip, eyeing him. Finally, dabbing at her lips with a napkin, she reached for his hand, pulling him up. "Come on, Calder. You need something to erase that frown."

He hadn't been frowning, had he? If so, only because the lighting in here cast her in the most glorious and flattering light. With her hand wrapped in his, he allowed himself to be led out onto the wooden dance floor.

She released him, standing and waiting.

"Oh," He realized his mistake, and heat flushed his face. Quickly, he took her into his arms, gently

94

wrapping one arm around her waist and another around her shoulder.

She lifted her arms to encircle around his neck, moving close until only the space of a few inches separated them.

Her exotic, bold and brassy floral scent swirled around him.

"Relax, Calder, I won't bite."

No, but he remembered the power she had when she attacked him with that baseball bat. She had been a formidable opponent then. He'd much rather dance with her now.

Leaning in, she rested her chin along his chest, near where his heartbeat wildly, and breathed a soft sigh.

Whatever reservations he held regarding River dissolved with that one soft sigh. Closing his eyes, Calder shifted his brain to the music, willing himself to move with it. Her body, firm in their battle, now softly meshed against his, was still strong but yielding. He could sense her strength and power, but her tender submission also delighted him.

Who knew River Gallagher could gently give in? What a wonderful surprise.

Despite her skill as a warrior and fierce protector, he found himself drawn to her, appreciating her fierce loyalty and her smooth self-confidence. The bling was optional, he supposed, but he could not deny River was a woman who knew what she wanted from life. And she was not afraid to reach out and grab it.

He was a respecter of that courage and philosophy. He could feel his body reacting, wanting to feel more of her softness. He swallowed heavily.

****

The music ended, the song slowly fading. River pulled herself away, looked into his eyes, felt her lips parting, and her pulse skip. He looked like he might kiss her. Would he really? She considered the option and was startled to feel warmth coursing through her. She licked her lips. Did she want a kiss from him?

Suddenly, he cleared his throat, nodding toward the table. "Our food has arrived."

Like cool water splashing over her, she jerked. "Yes." Free of his arms now, she walked stiffly to the table, took her seat, and reached for the wine glass. Too bad she was driving today, as she might need two glasses.

They ate in silence, lost in their own thoughts. The fish was tender and flaky, and the chips cooked to perfection. The wine was good, mellow, and offered a refreshing lift. Although he stated he wasn't hungry, Calder finished his whole meal. Perhaps it was just a good diversion from his thoughts of what was to come next. Did he think about what almost happened out on that floor just now? Even still, her body had not returned to normal settings. She shoved away the empty plate and blew out a low breath. "Ready? It's almost quarter of two."

He rose and pulled out her chair.

She walked at his side outside into the salt air. She wanted to keep a part of the magic they just shared but sensed the heaviness coming from Calder. Wordlessly, she reached out and wrapped her hand around his. When his wide-eyed gaze met hers, she simply smiled. The tears in her throat prevented her from speaking.

Chapter Seven

Calder supposed luck favored them. When he and River arrived, a good ten minutes early, his hand still vibrated from where River had held it. He couldn't shake her doe-eyed smile. He appreciated her compassion, but now it was time to get down to business.

Glazer, the man who ran the funeral home, met them and quietly ushered them to his office. Withdrawing some documents, he handed them over to Calder.

"This was the arrangement your father set up," he explained. "I have already spoken with Reverend Rutledge, and a memorial service in Sweetwater can be scheduled as soon as Wednesday or Thursday, if that sounds good."

Calder nodded tightly, passing back the papers. He'd already read his father's copy and discussed the plans during his first night back. Sitting here in this paneled room just made knowing the facts harder to accept. Glazer's compassionate smile didn't help much either. He sighed. "That would be fine. Either one."

We'll plan for Thursday then. Say, one o' clock?"

"Yes, fine."

"At the marina in Sweetwater Harbor?"

He closed his mind to the pictures circling through his mind. "Yes."

Glazer made a note on his papers.

Calder heard the pen scratch. The dry scratch sounded as parched as his throat felt.

"In that case, would you like a few moments to see the body one last time? To say goodbye?"

Did he? No, he remembered everything clearly enough already. The blood, the stillness in the room, the paleness of his face. The empty, vacant eyes. Finding no pulse. "No, thank you." He wished for some water. Or more wine. Did they have a fountain?

"I do." River passed Calder the slightest of glances and stood straight and tall, her lower lip quivering.

Again, he found himself respecting that bravery, how she held such loyal affection for his father. Even now, death had not dulled her allegiance. No wonder his dad loved her like a daughter.

"This way, please," Glazer said.

She squeezed Calder's shoulder and took a step, faltering. She blinked fast.

He saw the obvious difficulty she clearly experienced. He knew how she felt, like he could barely trust himself to walk. His throat burned. How much worse did she feel? He slid a hand over hers, smiling as she inhaled and turned to him with rounded eyes. What were her thoughts? "Ready?" he asked, his voice gentle as he lifted his chin toward the decorated walnut doors before them.

She nodded.

With a hand holding hers and the other lightly pressed in the small of her back, he gently supported her as he guided her to the shiny casket along the wall. He slowly lifted the lid. He closed his eyes and looked away, but he heard River's intake of breath. As his stomach rolled, he squeezed her hand reassuringly.

"I'm sorry," she whispered. "I had not thought his face was injured." She pressed one tightly balled fist to her mouth. "Someone will pay dearly for this."

"I am sorry, Miss Gallagher. I should have warned you." Glazer stepped back.

A moment later, she nodded.

He lowered the lid, clasping his hands in front of him. "Now, Mr. Finn, would you like the standard urn or something special?"

Another decision. He bit back a groan. Would they never end? "Just the standard one is fine." River rested a hand on his shoulder, and those familiar sparks passed between them again. His body automatically tightened in response to her touch.

"Go for something special, please? You might want to keep a little of their ashes for yourself. Both of them, together."

Or she might. He could gift her with a mixture. Or something. Nodding, he turned back to Glazer. "Maybe something in wood. Walnut perhaps?"

Her fingers tightened around his shoulder, and his breath hitched. He had no business responding to her empathy only feet away from his dad's coffin. Mentally, he told himself to shake off the spikes of interest darting through him, but the fact remained, he rather liked her touch. He could fall into those doe-big eyes of hers and drown.

He might be many things, but he knew he'd misjudged River Gallagher badly and did not deserve her compassion now. However, that miscalculation didn't mean his male hormones weren't letting him enjoy them, for as long as she offered.

****

River tackled the counter with a fierce scrubbing, her lips quivering. Once more their dinner was done and all that remained was the cleaning. The police called just as she and Calder were finishing, stating they concluded enough of their investigation so Calder could arrange for an escort into the house tomorrow. Long enough to look around, see if anything was missing, make a complaint if necessary, and gather a few things if he needed to.

Immediately after the call, he placed his plate in the sink and slipped outside.

His departure left her alone. Alone with her tangled thoughts and whispering heart. And not sure how to reconcile them.

One thing was for sure, she decided, blowing out a breath heavy enough to lift her bangs, attacking the counter with the dishrag was not going to help much. Maybe she needed fresh air instead. Sometimes, she needed the cool breezes to clear away the tangles and clutter in one's mind. Putting fresh coffee on to brew, she glanced outside, planning her route, and paused.

Calder sat on one of the Adirondack chairs on the back porch, staring out at the ocean.

In the twilight, under the rising moon, his face shone somber and thoughtful. Instantly, her heart lurched, touched by his silent pain. Pouring the coffee into two mugs, she added a liberal splash of caramel flavoring and stirred them. Then, sucking in a shaky breath, she pushed open the glass door and stepped into the night air. Salt and mint greeted her, and she saw Calder turn in his chair. The look he gave her nearly made her drop the mugs.

****

Calder sat in the chair, watching the gathering darkness, listening to the waves washing onto the sandy shore, and inhaling the salt-infused in the air along with the native horsemint growing among the wild grasses.

Well, now he could return to the house tomorrow, under police escort. He snorted. If he hadn't been insulted adequately already, their demeaning protocol would surely do it. At least they allowed him enough time to take inventory and see if anything was stolen during the event. He wondered why they were taking so long in their investigation. He grimaced over the loose term of investigation. The whole process seemed rather backward, but he was no expert on police things like inquiries.

At least, he could retrieve his car. They searched everything carefully and determined, in their examination, that it had no part in the events. *Go figure.* They were brilliant. He'd expected that little bit of freedom would excite him, instead it worked the opposite way. The suggestion that he soon would be allowed to return to the house to stay did not fill him with any great anticipation either.

What was the matter with him?

Hearing toenails clicking, he turned. The terriers clattered up, pausing, and sniffing his hand briefly before they clacked over the wooden boards, heading for the sand below. Soon, the black dog was swallowed by the inky twilight and the white one became a misty shadow.

"Here." River pressed a warm mug into his hand.

The smooth ceramic felt good, and he welcomed the warmth, not aware of being cold. Mercy, he was messed up. Vanilla and caramel rose to greet him, blending with the horsemint blowing wild in the air.

"You don't have to go alone, you know." River stood a foot away, hands cradled around her mug. She leaned against the wood railing, the breeze lifting her blonde hair.

Her faded jeans molded to her legs like a second skin. Her expression was soft in the disappearing light, and the white glow reached from inside. He raised an eyebrow, lifting the mug to his lips.

"I could go with you."

He rolled around the offer. He witnessed her grief at the funeral home. She was as torn up as he was, if not more so. Her offer to go along puzzled him as much as it pleased him. She was generous, but certainly the trip would be painful as well. "That's nice to offer," he said. "But I don't want to impose any more. Or take you away from work at your office."

She shrugged and searched the beach, checking for the dogs and then back to his face. "I can spare some time away. I just imagine this is a hard trip and was simply offering, in the spirit of friendship, that I accompany you." Again, she shrugged. "If you would rather I not go, that's fine. You know the way." She lowered herself to the other chair beside him, shoulders straight as she took a sip.

Her words ended in a tough barb, and he bit back a grin. She could change in midstream, leaving him lost—in so many ways.

The dogs returned, panting. Pepper went to River, whining for her scratch. Salty amazed him by going instead to Calder and sitting politely at his feet, one paw raised in a mute appeal for a pat. River shot him a disbelieving glance, her jaw agape and eyes rounded.

Warily, he reached out and gave the white dog a single stroke.

He remained, stubby tail wagging.

Calder shifted his gaze to River's, then back to the dog, giving it a couple more pats around his scruffy ears.

"You just made a friend," River said slowly. "He doesn't take to many new people."

Grinning, he looked back at River. "Tomorrow, if you could spare a little time, coming with me would be nice. Thanks." He suspected he made a couple of new friends tonight, River and her dog.

****

"Wow, the mess is worse than I had expected." River slowly turned in a circle in Frank's living room. "This looks like a war of some kind."

The mess looked exactly as Calder remembered. All except for the yellow police tape fluttering in the breeze outside. Standing with his hands balled into fists, he couldn't stop his gaze from going to the spot where his father's body had last lain. He pulled his hands out from the pockets and rubbed away the goose bumps that still rose despite the thick sweater he wore.

"Who do you think did this?"

He shrugged and wished he knew.

"What do you think they were after?"

He shook his head and wished he knew the goal, too. But he was clueless as the police on both questions.

Clapping her hands and expelling a deep breath, River surged forward and grabbed a lightweight entry table. She set it back in its place along the wall. Next, she picked up the flowerpot and brass figurine that had been there and replaced them, frowning at the broken branches on the white chrysanthemum. "What a shame, that was such a lovely plant." She gently fingered the soft leaves.

He stared for a moment, surprised by her grief at something as minor as a broken plant. How was this really affecting her? So much more damage than a broken plant surrounded them. He stepped over to another upended table, righting it. Rocking on three good legs, the desk wobbled, and the small drawer slid open. A magazine and a long, white envelope fluttered to the floor. Steadying the table, Calder reached for the envelope, recognizing the handwriting instantly. "Hey, River, this is for you." He handed it over and watched her face as she too recognized his dad's penmanship.

She turned over the paper. "It's sealed."

At the obvious remark, he grinned. "Aren't you going to open it?" He got the table balanced with the magazine and stepped aside, watching her.

"Should I?"

"It's made out to you." He shrugged. "Guess that means it's yours now." He paused, hands going to his pockets again. "But aren't you curious about what it might say?"

"Are you always like this about sealed things?"

He blinked. "Like what?" Considering how impulsive she could be at times, he figured she would rip the seal, yank out whatever was inside, and consume it. Apparently not.

She wagged the letter toward him. "Impatient to open sealed items? Are you this way with Christmas and birthday gifts or cards?"

Was he? He shifted. Not normally. But he

supposed he could be though. Couldn't most people be? When was the last time he'd received a surprise of any sort from someone? It had been a while. Brody wasn't the sort to remember or do much with gifts so that pretty much was the extent of people close enough to bother.

"Okay, you got me curious now," River sank into the only chair still upright. Hooking a fingernail under the seal, she ripped it.

The sound of tearing paper echoed through the still room. Oh, he got her curious now? Another sudden change of direction from Miss River Gallagher. He waited, rocking back on his heels, curious despite himself.

She pulled out two pages of white notebook paper.

He could easily recognize his dad's scrawled penmanship on both sides.

Before she was through the first paragraph, she was already sniffling, blinking back tears.

Fear lodged in his throat in a hard knot, and Calder rushed to hand over a tissue box from where it lay on the floor. He met her moist gaze, and the air rushed out of his lungs. "I'll go check the bedrooms."

"Thanks."

Shuffling away, he heard the rustling of paper again. A guttural sob shook the air, and he rushed away, unable to hear any more.

****

Drawing in another ragged breath, River told herself she could read this. Blinking fast, she started again.

My dearest River,
It has been one of the greatest joys of my life to

105

watch you grow up into the wonderful woman you are today. You are so intelligent, resourceful, beautiful, brave, and absolutely fearless in your quests. Anyone would be honored to be called your friend. I have been doubly honored in that I have also called you my trusted business partner. I can also call you the daughter I never had. And your parents have been gracious enough to let me think they've loaned you for all these years.

She stopped again, heaving in a ragged breath and wiping the moisture building in her eyes, then resuming.

But, River my dear, one thing has been lacking for you—true love. Yes, you have dated but nothing of merit or substance has ever come from them. My heart has ached as I see you reach so much success in your life, but never find that love worthy of your heart and soul. So my dying and final wish, my last wish, is that you find that one true love destiny meant for you to have and share.

"Yet, I fear this will be a journey, River. A journey from where you are now, content and secure, to a place of unwarranted trust. I can only hope and pray you are up to this journey. Because you will have to make it largely alone. That is why I fear and dread you won't attempt this search, my dear River. I fear you won't see the value of having the true love of another in your life and, therefore, will not devote the time to discovering the many joys. I pray I am wrong about this assumption for I want nothing else for you.

"So, please trust me when I say it will be worth it in the end if you can search your heart and find the courage I know you possess to make this journey I wish

for you.

All my love, always,
Frank

Carefully folding the letter, she held the pages tightly, staring out at the water, fist pressed to her mouth, and her shoulders slumped forward. Tightness filled her chest. Hot tears rolled down her cheeks. The ache… How had Frank seen into her soul to view the pain her loneliness sometimes brought? She had never spoken a word of it to anyone. Her family didn't even know of her fear of finding a lasting love. Yet, dear Frank had.

****

Calder stopped at the threshold of his dad's bedroom. This room looked almost as bad as the living room. Clothes had been hastily yanked out of the drawers and now either draped over sides of the drawers or lay in haphazard piles on the floor. A few bottles were knocked from the shelves in the adjacent bathroom, their contents of cotton swabs and aspirin spilled on the linoleum. He sat on the bed and righted the nightstand collection. He adjusted the drawer and basket beneath. Inside the thick hardcover memoir book, he noticed a similar, long, white envelope. A cold shiver crawled down his spine as he read his name scrawled in familiar bold letters.

Like River's letter, this one too was sealed. He held it close and hesitated. Whatever was written in River's letter was emotionally upsetting. Was he up to the same possibility? She was a strong woman, and right now, he felt very weak in comparison. Perhaps this note was something to save for later. Clearly, his dad hadn't intended for him to have it right away. Or else he would have shared it by now. Satisfied with his logic, he slipped the envelope into his jacket pocket.

He walked over to the other room he briefly occupied. It did not look too bad, considering the rest of the house. The bedcovers were pulled back. Had he made the bed when he last slept in it? Honestly, he didn't recall. He'd been pretty upset that night and the next morning, arguing with his dad about his misguided loyalty toward River.

Wincing now, he could almost smack a hand to his forehead. Sometimes, he was such an idiot! He grabbed a few personal items and his travel bag and quickly exited the room. He'd check the rest of the house, get River, and leave. He wasn't ready to stay here much longer.

Going back to his dad's room once more, he checked the closet. Up on the shelf was the embossed oak urn holding his mother's ashes. Carefully, he pulled down the smooth, rounded urn and placed it in the center of his bag, nestled inside soft cotton sweaters. He made one final check to see if anything else was missing: papers, documents, or pictures. The only thing he could think of was the big safe in his dad's office.

Ironically, that room was virtually untouched. The safe was still locked, apparently no one tried to break in. Well, whoever entered the house hadn't been after legal documents or deeds or valuables.

That was interesting.

Returning to the living room, bag in his hand, he glanced around. The rest of the mess would just have to wait until later.

River sat in the chair, her letter folded in her lap, tears brimming in her eyes as she stared out to sea.

He cleared his throat and adjusted his grip on the bag. "Ready?"

She jumped. Then she looked at his luggage, and her brows knit into a frown. "Aren't you staying here? Don't you want to straighten up more? I could help with that, really."

He shook his head. "No, this cleanup can all wait 'til later." Reaching for her hand, he offered her a lift. "I'd rather take you home instead."

She slowly smiled, accepted his hand, and stepped into his arms.

The hug spoke volumes and said all the words his aching heart could not say. For the first time, Calder wondered if he had genuine feelings for River.

****

Two days later, and back in his best suit and tie, with jeans aside for now, Calder stood quietly on the sand. The weather was typical Sweetwater Harbor: cold, cloudy, and miserable, but he seemed to be the only one noticing the weather. Around him were the collective residents of Sweetwater Harbor, filling the beach in their black sweaters, suits, and dresses. Beyond him, boats bobbed on their mooring lines, and above him sea birds cried and cawed. Beside him stood River and the Gallagher clan.

He met Raine, the youngest daughter and an attractive girl, just this morning. She brought both a pie and a sheet cake to the house, saying they would come in handy later.

Offering her condolences and a bite-sized cupcake, she went to join her parents.

Now, the five of them stood near the reverend as he spoke.

Shoulders hunched to the cold, River bit back the sobs as the sermon went on.

Calder knew she tried extremely hard to hold it together, and he appreciated her even more. This morning, over breakfast, coffee and preparing, she'd been subdued and distracted. He wondered how much the funeral upset her, how much was his dad's note, and how much she involved him as a house guest.

As he listened to the reverend extol his parents' many fine virtues, Calder stared at the ornate wooden urns placed side by side on the platform, flanked by flowers. Soon, eventually, the urns would be opened, and he would send the contents into the sparkling blue waters of the harbor, where they would perhaps drift out into the open ocean—his mother and father together again. He considered what a love they had that his dad kept his deceased wife's ashes all these years just for this occasion. What a love that he honored those vows they made however many decades ago. He was almost jealous he never experienced such a strong emotion. Whatever he felt for Penelope was certainly nowhere near this caliber.

What did he feel for Penelope? Planning their prenuptials was just as involved as planning the ceremony. But did he really want to spend eternity in a jar together? Would he remarry should something unfortunate happen during their marriage?

He glanced over at River, seeing a bastion of strength. Good thing she was so strong, or else he might become a basket case. He knew he was expected to be the one to release the ashes, but this morning he asked if she wanted to assist him. He almost asked what was in the letter but reconsidered. He had yet to read his own letter. Glancing now, seeing the moisture building on her lashes, noticing her lip quivering, he reached out his hand, taking her gloved hand into his.

She looked at him, blinking through her tears. Then, she offered him a smile that reached past the cold wind and touched his heart.

The reverend finished speaking and invited residents to step forth with their own comments.

Cordell and Muriel, their hands linked, stepped forward as one and turned to the crowd. Cordell spoke of their long friendship with Frank and Lola Finn, of having them as neighbors for thirty-two years.

Calder listened, hearing the pain of losing someone so close in such a tragic way.

Others slowly moved up, sharing their experiences with a man who was clearly the salt of the earth and his wife who was the light of his life.

He thought of how easy to think these people were talking about someone other than his parents. Why had he never seen them like this? Why had he never been a part of this glowing family? Oh, but he had, he just hadn't known or appreciated it at the time. He had missed that opportunity. Regret tasted bitter.

Now that he was grown and looking back, he could kick himself. He enjoyed a good childhood here, and he certainly loved his parents. He knew unquestionably they loved him. The sight of their urns now drilled at his heart. Feeling suffocated here in Sweetwater Harbor, he wanted more out of life than this little burg could ever offer. He wanted to see places and experience things. He wanted to live, which was something he thought he could never do here. Yes, he certainly could be an idiot sometimes.

No way could he miss the suspicious glances sent his way by the residents today. Some he already met, now with their families and children in tow, others he was clueless who they were. But they all knew him, and to judge by their expressions, they shared a different opinion of him than they had his father. Sadly, a harsher opinion.

All because he wanted to bring some modernization to this little burg. Was that desire now causing the animosity he saw on their faces? Would that be enough to make one of them break into his father's house and ransack it, beating and killing his father in the process? Could one of these grieving residents have played a hand in his dad's death, making him now the prime suspect?

****

River studied the citizens, most of them she had known all her life. She could not help but catch the undercurrents of distrust in their suspicious glances at Calder. Well, in a way, he brought that hostility on himself. If he had been a little more discreet about his plans and more sympathetic about people's lives and livelihoods, they might be more compassionate toward him now. They were only looking to protect what they had with Frank. She could not fault them.

However, she could fault them if one of them had anything to do with harming Frank. She recalled the bruising on his face, and chills covered her. The images still left her almost dizzy to think of what must have happened in that house while she was out with Calder. If only she could have been with Frank instead, when the riffraff came to call. She would have taken care of him...or her...or whoever. That would probably be one of her highest-ranking regrets for the rest of her life. A lump caught in her throat, and tears stung her eyes. She swallowed the lump and swiped at her tears. Nothing could erase the regret burning her heart.

Finally, with the residents finishing their own reflections, the reverend called Calder to come forth for the urns.

Keeping his hand wrapped around River's, he led her across the sand to the podium. Handing her one urn, he took the other. Nodding, he gave her a small smile. "Ready?"

Wordlessly, she nodded, blinking fast.

"Leave a little bit," he whispered as he approached the water's edge. "A couple of handfuls."

A warm relief spilled over her as she took in his message. He heeded her suggestion after all. Wisely, he chose to say no words to the crowd. What would be the point? Instead, he twisted open the urn, waiting for her to do the same. Simultaneously, gazes on each other, they knelt in the sand, hands cupped around their urns to gather the ashes.

Her heart constricting, River poured the gray ashes into the water, keeping back a couple handfuls. Lip quivering uncontrollably and hot tears spilling to the ocean below, she watched as the water swirled around the two lines of gray, blending them into one and gently carrying them back out into the waves.

She stood, dizzy with grief as she followed the gray spots out to sea. How was she supposed to carry on without her rock? Without Frank?

Chapter Eight

Darkness still lay heavy outside when Calder awoke the next morning. He shivered in the cold air. Did it ever get warm here? No, temperatures stayed cool even with the heat of summer, somehow, which was when Atlanta sweltered in the triple digits. Slipping out of bed, he padded into the living room, settling into a chair by the window with a blanket over his shoulders and his father's letter in his hand. He turned on the overhead lamp.

Holding the letter, still unopened, he fingered the paper, turning it over and over. He sniffed the paper, but no scent rose. His heart beat unevenly. He was scared to read it as he worried what his reaction would be. Suddenly, he heard the clatter of nails on wood and a soft woof. Looking down, he saw Salty at his feet, one paw raised to rest on his knee, tail wagging. "Why do you like me so much, dog?" he whispered, reaching out to pet the shaggy head. "I don't like dogs, remember?"

Undaunted, Salty stretched, reaching up both paws to Calder's knee and suddenly bounded into his lap.

Shocked, he lifted his hands into the air, and he barely kept his grip on the letter. "Hey! What are you doing?"

Unfazed, Salty settled in, stretching out on Calder's lap, his stumpy tail wagging as he closed his eyes.

"Good grief," he muttered, eying the scruffy

terrier. Nonetheless, he dropped his hands and stroked the fur, surprised to find it soft beneath the exterior scruffiness. Within moments, he was amazed to find his heart now slowed to a comfortable, reasonable calm. "Did you know you could do that, Salt?" He turned over the envelope once more, sighing deeply. Since he was here, he might as well read it now.

Salt raised his head to watch Calder as he broke the seal and pulled out the sheets. Then Salt whined once and lowered his head again, falling instantly asleep.

"Must be nice," Calder muttered, envious of the easy sleep. Pretty soon he would need sleeping pills. Still, maybe reading the letter would help. Or maybe not.

Dear Calder,

Son, I have followed your life and your career over the years with pride. You have done so well for yourself. Your mother and I both cried when you left us that day, but we also both knew you would never be content to stay here in Sweetwater Harbor. At least not until you had the chance to spread your wings and grow. And you have done that, son. You should be proud of yourself. We are.

His parents were proud. To see it in the black and white of his father's own hand felt good. They cried? Somehow, he never suspected that possibility. Mom maybe, but Dad? Pride stirred in his heart.

But the letter held more.

I remember when I first met your mother, Calder. She was a sparkly, little, brown-haired beauty from County Galway in the Old Country. She could light up a room just by walking into it. She had a laugh and a smile that made me almost fall to my knees. But she was also proud and determined. You have those same characteristics, son. You got them from her, for sure.

For me, it was love at first sight. The moment I first spotted her at the bridge in Galway, I was as hooked as a fish. I had been fishing, and she came along on her bicycle. She made me work a lot longer to convince her she loved me in return. She had the saltiest tongue and the sharpest wit, and she used both against me like a twin-edged sword.

Calder could almost hear his dad's chuckle. He could also picture the young lovers meeting at an Irish stone bridge. Clearing his throat, he read on.

Now I would not have traded the years I spent with your mother for all the gold in Ireland. She completed my life. Her spirit, her fire, and her passion, they drove me crazy, but I would not have had her any other way. She was the other half—the one who made me a whole man. And that, Calder, my boy, is what I wish for you.

A lasting love that fills those empty spaces in your heart. You have no spark in your life, no one to confound you, leave you mesmerized and enchanted beyond all words. I hope you can one day stop running and stay long enough to find that special love. If she makes you even half as happy and complete as your mother made me, my final wish will be granted, and you will be one incredibly happy man.

But remember this, son: don't ever confuse complacency for contentment. They are not the same thing. Sometimes, complacency is only a mask for fear to step out. I soon learned to savor your mother's attitude like a starving man savors a home-cooked meal.

Calder heard that chuckle in the air—in the

stillness of the room. Goose bumps rose along his arms.

Salty raised his head, peering with his black eyes, wagged his tail again, and returned to sleep.

Calder moved to another page and continued.

So, my son, with the end soon at hand, I cannot express how glad I am you returned home. But now that you are here and will soon get this letter, I pray with it comes a hope and sincere desire to step out of your complacency of success and search for the maiden who will complete your heart. I hope she is every bit as strong and courageous deep in her heart as you have been as you chased your dreams. Then you two can make new dreams come true together.

With much love,

Your father

Folding the letter, he carefully put it back in the envelope, as the air left him. Outside the window, dawn was breaking. He reached up to switch off the light, smiling at the snoring dog in his lap before turning to watch the early morning fishermen chug out to sea.

In his heart, he took a slice of comfort in hoping his parents were together once again at that stone bridge in Galway. He smiled, picturing them flirting and kissing like it was their first meeting.

He hoped they got a fresh start at happiness again. He had not been the best child for them, and he regretted his selfish actions. He wished he could go back in time and be the son they deserved. Maybe one day he would have a son, or a daughter, and he could have the child he should have been.

****

River stretched and yawned, reaching out to pet the dogs.

Pepper peered at her, panting.

"Where's Salty?" Rolling out of bed and tugging on her robe, she headed for the living room, Pepper trotting at her heels. Reaching the doorway, she slammed to a halt, one hand going to her chest.

Bathed in the morning glow, Calder sat at the window, looking out beyond the harbor.

Salty curled in his lap.

The scene was altogether tender and poignant. Then, she spotted the envelope gripped in his hand, and she knew Frank's letter to his son had been as emotional as hers.

Swallowing hard, she nodded to the terrier at her feet and stepped into the room. Crossing to the chair, she waited until Calder looked up. "Hi," she greeted him. "New buddy?" She flicked a finger at Salty.

"He just hopped up here on his own."

"I don't doubt it. It's hard to make him do anything he doesn't want to do. He was a real challenge to obedience train." She gazed out over the harbor. "Looks like it might be a nice day out."

She saw his shrug in the glass reflection, and her heart twisted in sympathy.

"Are you okay?" She turned back toward him and took a hesitant step forward.

He nodded. "Yeah, just thinking. You know."

"Yes, I know." Frank's letter had a way of making one stop and think, a lot. She rested a hand on his shoulder for a moment. "Do you have any plans for the day?"

"Not at the moment."

"How about I go make breakfast? Then after showers, we can figure out the day's game plan."

"Sure."

River took her time, first running Pepper out for a short walk. Salty would move when he wanted to, and she would bet not until Calder got up. Finished with the Scottish terrier, she went into the kitchen, looking around. Eggs, pancakes, or waffles, what should she make?

Pausing, she braced her hands against the counter, suddenly out of breath. Why was the sight of Calder sitting by the window, bathed in dawning light, so gripping? Enough to leave her almost trembling and breathless?

Could the reason be because every time she looked into his eyes, she saw the eyes of his father instead? She supposed that was possible. Or was she seeing the man young Calder had grown into?

Maybe she needed a diversion. Maybe she had been spending too much time with him. The last few days they had hardly been apart. Well, he had his rental car back now, so she was free of the transportation duties. Not that she minded them, of course. And her plan to take him around to the area residents no doubt gave him some other things to hopefully think about, beyond his dad's letter. But now maybe she needed to return to her other duties.

She hauled sausage and eggs out of the fridge, certain she had the perfect diversion for herself.

****

Calder was halfway to the house when River caught him on the stairwell.

"Would you mind if I went back to the office today?" she asked.

He paused, taking in her damp hair and breathing

119

in her clean fragrances. One was fruity and one was herbal, and one was spicy. What an intoxicating mix, coupled with fresh lip gloss and rosy cheeks. If he ran a fingertip over her skin, he would feel the satiny softness. She had painted fresh colors on her nails as well; they were strawberries with a dot of shimmer. Again, he felt that familiar hardening of his body's response. He tightened his hand around the wood banister, feeling its smooth finish.

He dragged his tangled mind off what she looked and smelled like and focused on her question. "Why would I mind? You have a business to run." He, of all people around, should understand the importance of running a business. If he didn't check in with his own business soon, Brody would have a fit.

"Well, I don't know. Just asking." She remained a moment before beaming a big smile. "In that case, if you need me, you know how to reach me. Just call Daphne."

"I'll be fine." He smiled. "I'll have the dogs for company." He glanced down at Salty, who seemed determined to follow him into the bathroom, and possibly the shower as well. He nodded at the little white dog. "Uh, is he often like this?"

"Nope, I've never seen him act this way before." She shrugged. "Something about you and him clicking, I guess. He's always been his own kind of dog."

Spinning with her hair twirling, she ambled down the hall.

Her perfume lingered in her wake. Sure enough, as soon as she closed the front door, the black dog retired to her bed and curled up, chewing a bone.

Salty sat at Calder's feet, his tongue lolling to the

side.

He shrugged and breathed in a deep lungful of River's intoxicating blend of scents before it faded, then he and the terrier went into the bathroom.

"But you're staying out of the shower, just so we're clear, dog."

****

River was a little disappointed more things were not waiting to be done at Watercolors. She found Daphne hard at work at her desk, and her calendar empty. "No appointments? Really?" she asked, resignation in her tone. She reached out her hand. "I'll get you fresh cocoa then."

Daphne held out her cup. "I think people just wanted to give you some time to settle before making demands."

"Maybe I need demands made on my time," she muttered, walking away before Daphne could hear her.

"So, how is it going with Calder Finn staying on with you?" Daphne asked.

She returned with the steaming mug. His name still rolled off her tongue sounding like a fish part, making River bite back a grin. "Fine," she said quickly. "He's actually the perfect house guest."

Daphne leveled a stare.

The kind that must have made third and fourth graders cringe when she taught, before retiring four years ago. But her words were true, she could not ask for a better house guest. She met Daphne's dubious stare. "Salty loves him," she volunteered. "The silly dog has practically adopted him."

Daphne sniffed and returned her attention to her cocoa.

River retired to the office and pondered the rest of her day. She could take out the boat, or she could go visit her family or see Raine. But what she needed was action, activity, an outlet for her churning emotions from Frank's letter, her grief, and Calder's very real presence. "I've got it!" She snapped her fingers. "I know where I can go. It is way past time, too." Leaping up, she entered the lobby where Daphne was busy with a stack of files. "If anyone calls or needs me, I'll be out of town. Down at the site."

Stopping at the restaurant just before leaving town, she grabbed a sandwich, chips, and coffee to go, then she crossed the drawbridge out of town. Getting out of town was just what she needed. She lowered the window just enough to let in some fresh air. A little physical activity to get her mind off things and help her move on. Like her dad said, sometimes you needed to look at things from other people's perspective to appreciate what you have in yours.

****

Calder returned from his beach walk with both dogs and checked his phone. No new messages. Well, the silence was okay. That meant nothing new had come up requiring him to deal with. Good. He still wasn't up to making decisions. He'd found a flying disc in the back yard and, after idly tossing it, discovered his new buddy Salty was a natural canine flying machine, crazy to get the disc. Half an hour later, he set aside the disc and took both dogs for a walk instead, feeling the sunshine beating down on him.

He planned on checking on city zoning ordinances but somehow lacked the ambition right now. He could do half a dozen things that required his attention, but he just could not work up the energy or enthusiasm. So now, lacking motivation, he pondered what to do with the rest of his day. He could arrange to pick up dinner from town and surprise River. She might like that since she had been cooking a lot. And his cooking was best made in the form of reservations.

Brody often teased him about how most the city's restaurants were on his auto dial and rated between delivery and pick-up service. He argued that since they tended to work such long hours, he needed a steady supply of food providers. He made a fist, feeling emotions gripping him like a vise again. He missed Brody! He missed him like a brother and a friend. Right now, he needed Brody close.

Salty nosed his leg and whined.

"You're right, little buddy. I need Brody back at the firm to keep it running. People might have a cow I'm not there, but at least they have Brody, and he'll love the double workload." He patted the terrier's soft head and smiled. "Right now, I have your mama to think about. And our dinner tonight."

Giving the dogs each a bone, he headed out to his car, now parked in her driveway. First, he would stop at Watercolors and see what she wanted and what time would be good, then he could go place the order and pick it up later. He walked through the door.

Daphne sorted through a stack of letters and magazines. She glanced at him and returned to her task, her lips thinning. "She's not here," she said, not bothering to look up.

He kept a respectful distance, keenly aware of her distrust and her quiet disapproval. What he ever did to her since he had no idea who she was. "Well, is she nearby? I have a quick question."

"She's gone for the day, working on a building development project."

He perked up. Had he heard right? River could build and develop something? Here in town? Since when? River Gallagher creating something was a truth he would have to see to believe, no offence to Daphne. "Where is she?" he prompted as she continued to ignore him. "I'll go see her about my business." She looked at him for the first time, a level, hard stare that he felt with all the force of a bulldozer.

"She's out of town."

Really? That figured. He blew out a frustrated breath, more curious. To hell with the consequences. "I can always hitch the horse to the carriage to get there," he said dryly. "Do you have an address?"

She frowned but reached for a scrap of paper and pen and scribbled a line on it. Passing it over, she caught and held his gaze. "Don't hurt her," she warned evenly, enouncing each syllable distinctly.

"Ma'am, I would never dream of it." The way he saw it, the chances were much more tilted in her favor. Instead of explaining, he glanced at the paper. *227 Goldenrod, Sullysville*. He smiled and waved the note. "Thank you."

Exiting, he jogged back to his car and programmed the address into the global positioning system, eager for the directions. South, of course, where he might encounter the drawbridge up. Turning the key, he turned south. First, a coffee for the road. He wasn't supposed to drive out of town, but Sullysville wasn't that far out of town. He'd take his chances with the law.

****

"River, it's great to see you again!"

"It's good to be back, Dot." She smiled as she looked around the charity housing home. Walls were all up now, and doorways trimmed. Bedrooms and bathrooms already had doors hung. "This place is coming along nicely, isn't it?" Each time she visited a construction site, she was amazed at how something could go from an idea to drawings and then to blueprints and finally to concrete and wood and windows. So much had been completed since her last visit. "The windows are in now too."

"Yes, as of late last week. Come inside. You'll be pleased. Are you here to work?"

She smiled, already taking her coat off. "I sure am, if you have a job for me."

Following Dot, she skirted other site workers, busy with their own tasks and piles of building materials. She felt a surge, knowing she had been a driving part in starting this project and in making a difference for someone.

"We can always find willing workers something to do." Once inside, Dot led the way to a back room, where the drywall was taped and sanded and several cans of paint sat in the corner.

River read the color on the nearest can. "Dolphin aqua. That's a nice shade," she commented. "It ought to look pretty when it's up."

Dot wore a huge smile, reached for a brush, and handed it over. "Yes, I believe it will. I'll come help you when I get a chance, okay?"

Half an hour later, River decided something was relaxing about painting a room. The work was both mindless and rhythmic. The dolphin aqua shade, a soft blue gray, reminded her of the waves when they were calm, washing ashore in quiet succession. Plus, she felt a real sense of satisfaction seeing the paint covering the walls. She filled her tray, loaded the brush again, and applied it to the wall in a sweeping arc. She might hurt like crazy later, but this activity was so worth it right now. Someone soon would sleep in this room with its tranquil walls.

Maybe this task was what she needed to do—go and paint her own house. She had lived there for five years and only painted it once. Maybe the time had come to do a complete color change. She liked her style and the look of the place, but the moment was right for something different. Raine decorated her little place in Asian design with bold colors, and it all looked nice. She preferred pastels and could do something maybe contemporary or at least modern.

When she got back to town, she could stop at the hardware store and pick up some paint samples and fabric swatches, just to play around with ideas. Then, once Calder was gone, she could start a remodeling project of her own.

Unless he wanted to stay and help. Her heart skipped a beat at the thought. They could have fun painting and decorating.

"River, hey, there's—Wow, this looks great."

River stopped, lowering her brush as Dot came in the room, changing sentences midway through.

"And you're a mess." Dot handed out a water bottle.

"Thanks." River took the bottle, knowing she always made a mess when she painted. She preferred to call it getting into her work. "So, what were you saying?"

"That some guy is here looking for you. He's back behind me somewhere." She jerked a thumb behind her.

Guy? Midway of twisting off the top, River stopped. She lifted her gaze to follow behind Dot and there stood Calder filling the doorway with sheer amazement on his face.

Her heart suddenly frisked ahead like smooth rocks skipping across the ocean's surface. "Calder, what are you doing here?"

****

Calder looked around, taking in the fresh paint both on the walls and her. At least it wasn't a bat this time. She looked positively...riveting with paint smeared on her face, streaked in her hair, and splattered on her clothes.

She changed clothes from this morning. Now, she was in torn jeans that hugged her legs and had both knees blown out, a blue Carolina sweatshirt, and a bejeweled ball cap to hold her ponytail out of the way. Of course, she still had to retain something with bling, even if just a ball cap.

Finally, he remembered what brought him here. "I had a question," he got out, glad to have found his voice. He coughed once. "Daphne said you were here working on some development project." What an understatement. "Why didn't you ever tell me you were involved with building affordable housing?" This discovery also explained the bumper sticker on her car that read, *Everyone deserves a place to call home.* He'd have to take a second look at her bumper and window stickers. What other causes did she support?

"You never asked. What does it matter?" She lifted

her shoulder in a shrug. "This is something I do in my spare time."

What did it matter? Good question. Somehow, knowing she volunteered, and with the dirty, messy part of it, made one more adjustment in his opinion of her. Helping a non-profit organization was a worthy endeavor and one that he usually sent a check to for their yearly fundraiser. He'd never felt the need to get dirty with the hands-on work. But River did.

Her friend cleared her throat, clapping together her hands.

The blush in her cheeks deepened and River raised her hand. "Dot Granger, this is Calder Finn. Dot is site leader here and this project is about the fifteenth house we've worked on together."

"Fifteen. Very impressive." Calder took her hand into his. Dot was unquestionably older than both him and River, but she was spry and quick to smile. "Are all of them right around here?"

Dot nodded. "Yes. But they're also over the three-county area, including two in Sweetwater Harbor."

His eyebrows shot up, and he looked to where River was drinking from her bottle. Her lips looked so pretty as they curled around the bottle's neck. He wanted to kiss those lips, but he dragged his attention back to Dot. "Two affordable houses are in Sweetwater Harbor?"

Dot nodded. "Yep, both over on the peninsula. We are thinking a third might be started before the end of next year."

"See, new growth is happening after all," River said quietly, capping her bottle and setting it aside. "Did you say you had a question? That brought you all the way down here?"

Dumbstruck with taking in both her wildly messy beauty, and the fact she had a philanthropic nature, and new houses were in town, he struggled to recall his question. "Dinner. Yes, I'm offering to bring dinner to the house tonight. I stopped at Watercolors to see what you wanted and when."

River blinked. "Dinner would be nice. Say around seven? Whatever you wanted to bring would be fine. Anything filling is good, I guess."

Surprise and gratitude crossed her blue-gray streaked face.

She swiped at the paint, smearing it more.

"Say, Calder, you wouldn't be interested in helping out, would you?" Dot touched his arm. "We can always use more manpower. If you have a few free moments, of course."

Now he blinked, surprised at the invitation. Looking to River, she had that cinnamon eyebrow raised, waiting. Dot's smile was hopeful. "What do you need done? I'm not exactly dressed for construction work." He dressed in jeans and a sweater, but he certainly had time on his hands right now.

"You're dressed fine for what we need." Dot curled her fingers around his arm and guided him to the open doorway. A big smile crossed her face as she chatted. "We could have you help with the shingling unless you don't do heights. Have you ever installed cabinets? Do you know plumbing by any chance? Then there's always helping River with the painting in here."

While that last suggestion held the most appeal, Calder allowed Dot to talk him into assisting two other men with hauling in cabinets to the kitchen and installing them, plus hooking up the kitchen sink. Exchanging handshakes and first names, Calder was soon part of the unofficial kitchen crew.

After the third time he brushed sweat out of his eyes, he paused for a breather. What would Brody think if he saw him like this? Instead of just writing checks, could he convince Brody into donating manual labor for the Atlanta charity homes?

Once again, he questioned whether he would return to Atlanta when he could or stay here.

****

River watched as Dot led him away and returned to her paintbrush, a strange hum vibrating through her. What just happened? She attacked the wall with fresh vigor, imagining why Calder would drive out of town, against police orders, to ask her wishes about dinner. Why didn't he just call her phone? Maybe he was stir crazy and wanted to go for a drive. Maybe he needed a distraction as much as she had. She swept the brush along and pictured his reaction to her volunteer project. Why the big shock?

She chuckled at the memory of his expression as Dot asked him to stay and help. She figured he would immediately, and politely, refuse. Instead, he agreed. Somehow, she expected him to be more the type to help a charity by handing out a tax-deductible check instead of rolling up his sleeves and grabbing a wrench.

But he had. And while he looked as mystified as she felt, River had to appreciate his efforts. Maybe he wasn't as bad as she sometimes thought he could be. She blew out a breath and lowered the brush, her arm aching. Well no wonder, the room was just about finished, and it did look good. She had to repaint her place, and this shade was calling out as a starting place. But first, lunch.

Going out to the car, she grabbed the sandwich and chips she'd brought from town. Others were starting their breaks, as well, as Dot went around tapping shoulders and handing out water bottles. Had Calder brought anything to eat? Doubtful since he had not expected to find her working on a charitable housing project. Glancing at the food in her hand, she headed for the kitchen. After turning the corner, she halted.

Calder and one of the older guys lay side by side on the floor, heads stuck under the sink as they worked on the pipes. The older guy apparently had done this before and was giving Calder instructions.

Resting her hand on the unfinished wall, River watched, feeling a tug in her chest as she listened to the conversation between the men. Within moments, she had to wipe away a tear.

She knew Jerry well and worked on a few houses together with him and his wife. Everyone in the room was quiet, hanging on Jerry's conversation as he told Calder about how they met, and loved working on these houses together. He was convinced their shared commitment to the charitable housing was part of what made their marriage so strong. He was also skilled in plumbing and shared the benefit of that experience with Calder, too.

Jerry's words were nothing new to River, but Calder's reaction was. He lay on his back on the floor, twisting pipes and pounding fittings, and hung on Jerry's every word.

She knew Tandy and Jerry had a good relationship, but how could a man who was marrying simply for convenience understand that basic truth? Would she ever marry for nothing but pure love like her parents had, like Frank and Lola shared, and like Tandy and Jerry enjoyed?

****

Calder gripped the wrench and concentrated on both the pipes above his head and the old guy beside him. Jerry said this house was the tenth he'd worked on and kept coming back for the satisfaction of seeing the homeowner get their keys. He grew up in substandard housing and wished a program like this existed when he was young.

Apart from that, Jerry also talked about his wife, Tandy, who was outside helping with the siding. Obviously, Jerry loved his wife and loved volunteering on the houses. The light in his eyes and the pride in his voice were enough to form lumps in Calder's throat. He told himself the mist in his eyes was from the pipe compounds in the jars, but he knew better.

He was also still a little startled at finding River here, dressed in paint, and amazed to find himself spread out on the floor like he was. What was happening?

"Hey, Calder, time for a break," River said.

Looking up, Calder saw her standing at the doorway. Had she been watching him? For how long? Didn't he make a sight down here? A few minutes ago he'd been on his hands and knees, twisting pipes. Had she witnessed that task, too? Warily, he climbed to his feet, brushing away the plastic shavings. He looked at his partner, still under the sink. "Jerry, I guess it's break time."

Jerry scooted out and stood, too. "I'll go hunt up

132

my beautiful bride. No doubt she packed a picnic for us."

Watching Jerry stride away, Calder could not mistake the older man's eagerness nor miss the pet name he called his wife. Suddenly, Calder felt a slash of jealousy knifing through him. No doubting that was what his dad had been referring to—that emptiness he sometimes felt and tried to ignore.

"Calder? Are you having a good time?"

"Yeah, I guess so." He looked around, more to avoid noticing all the paint smears now covering River like blue freckles. She was too adorable.

"Well, I brought lunch." She shook the paper bag in her hand. "I'll share."

Now that he thought about it, he did feel the beginnings of hunger pangs. "That's thoughtful of you. Thanks." He gave her a smile and reached for her arm. Warmth passed between them as he escorted her outside.

The sun's rays fell around them as he joined River on the partially completed porch.

Dot supplied fresh water bottles and moved on, leaving them alone.

Calder studied the foot-long, submarine sandwich River pulled from her bag. "You sure you got this in Sweetwater Harbor? I didn't know anyone in town made subs."

"What If does." She broke off half, handing it over. "Careful, it's got everything."

This What If place sounded like it merited another look around…as did the peninsula. He remembered it as a forlorn, desolate chunk of sandy soil occupied by seashore elder shrubs and sea life. Now homes stood there, with more forecasted. Who owned all this land? Him?

"Penny for your thoughts." River spoke up. "Aren't you enjoying yourself?"

Her comments made him aware he had been too quiet for too long. Oh, he was, more than he imagined he could. The only thing better would to have stayed in that bedroom and see how much paint River could get on the walls. "I am," he said. "Just thinking again."

"I was thinking, too," she said. "Of painting my house. Today sort of gave me the incentive to make a change or two. I really like this color."

He could tell, because she wore it nicely. He reached for a chip, chewing thoughtfully. The salt and cheddar cheese flavors tasted good on his tongue, and he savored the crunch. He liked her Southwest designs but figured she'd come up with something just as attractive. Design had never been his strong suit. He hired a design consulting group to decorate his condo and the office.

"So, what are you thinking of?" She reached for a chip once his hand was clear of the bag.

He should have lingered to see if she'd reach into the bag and touch his hand. "With the building going on in Sweetwater Harbor, I need to study the deeds and see what properties are on lands I now own."

River coughed and reached for the water bottle. "What?"

"Yeah, and this What If place sounds very progressive, as well. Maybe hope exists when we can get more broad-minded businesses welcomed in, once I see what land is available."

River slammed down the remains of her sandwich.

"That is most insulting!" She climbed to her feet. "I can't believe you would think of something mercenary now." Spinning, she strode inside. Soon, she was back on the porch. She spared him a disgusted huff before marching across the lawn to her car.

Mystified, Calder watched her back out onto the road and disappear.

Within minutes Dot walked over. "What happened with River?" she asked. "I've never seen her leave like that."

Feeling like the ground had just been ripped out from under him, he turned from where River disappeared and slowly faced Dot. "I have no idea."

Chapter Nine

River stopped long enough to swing by Sweet Obsessions and buy a half-sized Indulgence Tart from Raine. The item was one of her more sinful desserts that was extra heavy on the chocolate.

Raine's eyes twinkled as she packed up the requested treat. "What happened? You and Calder have a spat?"

"Not now," River warned her sister, holding up a hand. "I need a shower, not conversation."

"Better make it a cold one," Raine suggested dryly as she held out the sweet treat.

"Funny, sis. Ha." Spinning, she headed for the door. "Later."

Once home, she stripped off her paint-stained clothes, tossing them in a pile near the washer, and stomped to the bathroom in her underwear, not caring if Calder happened to show up.

How dare he! How dare he even think, let alone mention, researching property deeds to bring in business. Had she not been clear enough that Sweetwater Harbor did not want his kind of growth and commerce? Didn't he get that these people depended on her to keep life the way they knew during years with Frank as their landlord?

Did he have to ruin a perfectly wonderful day of the two of them working together on a charitable

136

house? His sense of timing was lousy, to say the least. How dare the man!

Ignoring her sister's advice, she stepped under the warm water, letting it sluice over her and wash away the paint and dirt. Finished, muscles already complaining of her workout, she filled the tub with fresh warm water, adding a few drops of lavender oil and a generous handful of Epsom salts. Armed with a terry bath pillow, she settled back into the warm abyss and sighed deeply.

The terriers perched at the bathtub edge, watching.

"If only Calder hadn't gone and ruined everything," she lamented to the listening dogs. "He'd looked so right, so handsome, helping Jerry in the kitchen. And I felt…something…watching him. I loved painting in the bedroom, knowing he was only a few rooms away. That's silly, I know, especially now, to envision the two of us working on a house together. Funny thing is, this house wasn't even ours. But for the two of us to be working together on a volunteer project just felt right. Together, you know."

She was glad she didn't expect the dogs to make sense of what she said, because it sure sounded mangled to her own ears.

Darn that Calder Finn anyway, why'd he have to go and ruin a perfectly good day and a perfectly good lunch? Sitting on the sun-warmed porch with him, the two simply sharing a sandwich and sunshine…and talking was so pleasant. Why did he have to drag progressive growth for the town into it?

Because she had asked what was on his mind.

She might not ever do that again.

****

Calder crept up the stairs and into the house, following the trail of shoes, socks, and finally a pile of clothes. Then the scent of lavender and the sound of water entered his awareness. He set down their supper on the counter as clicking nails told him his white furry buddy was coming from the bathroom.

Hadn't she closed the bathroom door? Apparently not.

"Hey, Salt," he greeted the terrier. "So, how mad is your mama?" Sinking into a chair, he was barely settled before the dog leaped into his lap. Chuckling once, he scratched his ears. "Because I think we might have crossed over from insulted to mad today."

He could never explain to Dot what happened, mostly because he didn't understand it himself. But he suspected her attitude had to do with how he answered her question. Once again, he suspected, he meant one thing, and she heard another. This miscommunication was getting to be a bad habit he wished they could break.

Staying at the project site, he helped Jerry until the job was finished. Then begging his leave, he returned to town, stopping to pick up dinner. Tempted to stop at What If, he chose instead to go to Bobbers for their dinner specials. One meatloaf and potatoes and one beef tips and noodles, he'd give her first pick. If she ever got all the paint washed off.

"You're back."

His head swiveled toward the sound of her voice. His heart skipped a beat. She stood in the room, a fuzzy purple robe tied around her waist, and Pepper at her feet. Her hair was wet but clean, hanging in wet tangles. She smelled of lavender and citrus. "I just got back a few minutes ago. I brought dinner from Bobbers." He motioned toward the Styrofoam containers on the counter. "Pick one, and I'll take the other."

"That was nice." She peeked inside them, selecting the meatloaf container. Sitting, she simply held it, looking out the window at the gathering darkness.

"Can we talk?" Calder asked. He reached out to stroke Salt. "Without exploding?"

She cut him a frown. "I didn't explode."

He bit down on his tongue. "So earlier, at the house, that display back at the housing project wasn't mad?"

"Maybe a little."

He'd sure hate to see a lot. "River, I apologize. I know what I said upset you, and I am sorry for that. I didn't mean for you to misunderstand what I was saying."

"You have a bad habit of incorrect speaking, Calder. Didn't they teach you how to talk in Atlanta?"

More the other way around, but no matter. "I'm from Atlanta, not Mars."

"No, you're from Sweetwater Harbor and currently live in Atlanta." Her arms crossed over her chest. "I think you occasionally vacation on Mars."

Wrapping his mind around that one, he noticed her small smile. Grinning in return, he had to admit it might seem that way to some. Yet, the longer he was here in Sweetwater Harbor, the easier he could forget about his life and concerns back in Atlanta. He'd have hell to pay with Brody at some point.

She lifted her wet hair, sighing. "Okay, so what were you saying earlier that you botched so badly? Your timing was super lousy, by the way."

He bit back a sigh of his own. Carefully, he constructed his answer. "I was thinking it's time I learned what the actual size of the properties technically are, since I don't recall the specifics. As trustee, you would know perfectly what everything is. So, when you have some free time, I would like to schedule an appointment to go over the legal descriptions and map them out."

"Map them out?" Her eyes narrowed at the term.

"Just an expression," He held his fingers splayed. "I mean to take an inventory, if you will."

She huffed. "Then just say an inventory, if that's what you mean."

"Of course. Take an inventory of the properties, the land, the buildings, and the rest of the assets as well. And stocks, bonds, certificates, and the like."

"Paper assets and coins are kept in Frank's house safe. The deeds to the real property are kept in the safe at my office. Copies of both are in a safe deposit box that we both have keys to."

"Okay." Now, this was what he called making real progress. "Later on, we can figure out a convenient time to go over everything and make an inventory. Maybe tomorrow I can go to the house, clean up a bit more, and check out the safe. It did not look like anyone tried getting in the safe."

She opened the lid of her dinner container.

Rich meaty aromas escaped with the steam. Hunger drove him to the counter where he gathered his dinner. The plate was hot under his hand, and beefy smells surrounded him as he sat with it balanced on his lap. He watched her take a bite and chew slowly.

"Which meant whoever broke in wasn't after

Frank's paper assets or coins."

He nodded. "Assuming he or she even knew they existed. For example, I never knew he collected any coins."

She looked up and blinked, her brows knit into peaks. "Frank has a nice coin collection. I don't know for sure it's worth offhand, but it has to be somewhere between modest and sizeable."

Calder rubbed his chin. "No one ripped the house apart looking for it. Who else would know about this coin collection?"

"I don't know." She shrugged. "Anyone who knew Frank. You know, really *knew* him. Enough to talk about stuff like that. Some people collect stamps, but he liked coins."

Not for the first time, Calder had to wonder how much about his parents he never knew. And it sure was looking like theft wasn't the perpetrator's reason for breaking in and killing his dad. So what was?

****

River didn't know if Calder would be home or not but was glad to see his car still parked in her driveway. All day she wondered if he would stay at her house or go back to Frank's. Scouting out the house, she found him in the back, wandering along the shore with the dogs playing in the sand.

Her heart skipped suddenly as she rushed down the steps to meet him. She came to a breathless stop beside him. "So, I have this suggestion," she said by way of greeting.

He lifted a brow and stepped back one pace. "What's that?"

"Some friends stopped by Watercolors today and

invited me to a beach dinner tomorrow night over on the peninsula. They're usually fun. Would you like to come along?" She watched him turn the invitation over in his mind. "I was thinking it might help snap you out of this depressing funk you're stuck in."

"I can't." He gave a wag of his head. "Or I shouldn't."

She drew back, tilting her head to study him. Slowly, she moved forward and touched his arm, as if to hold him close. "Why not? Do you have better plans?"

His brows arched briefly, his gaze held hers, then he shook his head again. "No, I don't. But pretty much everyone in this town hates me. So, I doubt they would appreciate me showing up at their dinner party."

He had a point, but she also knew her friends. When she mentioned Calder, they hadn't said either way whether he was welcomed. They knew he might come along, and they were okay with that. That's one reason why she liked her friends. "I am sure they'll be okay with it if you want to come along. You'd be coming as my...guest." She finished, hunting for the right word.

He smiled.

A look of amusement crossed his face. She pulled away her hand from his arm.

His gaze dipped to her hand and back to her face. "What would you say right now, River? Really?"

Heat flushed through her face, and she turned to the water, letting the cool salt air fan her. "I don't know. Guest works, though." She lifted the hair off her neck, realizing how close she came to saying "friend." Did he suspect her feelings? Glancing up, she saw only the amusement in his eyes. His smile did great things for his face. She didn't blame him for being blue, but she couldn't help but want to help ease his gloomy mood.

Sticking her hands in the pockets of her jacket, she turned back. "So, what did you do all day? Hang out with the dogs?"

"No, I went over to the house and cleaned up more stuff. Broken things, and some papers and small items thrown about. Things are looking decent now." He sighed and raked a hand through his dark hair. "I didn't find any more letters."

"Good," she said. "I'm not sure I can handle another one like the first one."

"Yeah." He blew out a heavy breath, and his gaze moved around.

River thought he felt the same way. She wondered what was in his letter and if it hurt him as much as Frank's touched her.

"I also went through the contents of the safe. Indeed, the coin collection is extensive. I left it for safekeeping. In time, I can take it to a dealer back in Atlanta to find out its worth. I found the house keys up on a dusty shelf, and I locked the doors behind me. I assume you have a set of your own."

"I do." She swung her gaze around the house, as if it might be hanging on a hook some place. She nibbled her bottom lip for a moment and then gave him an apologetic smile. "Somewhere. So do Mama and Daddy, though it's questionable if they know where theirs are. I don't think we used them much."

His lips thinned, and he stared out at the water for a moment before turning back.

She took the time to study his strong profile.

"How was your day?"

"Fine, the usual kind of routine things."

He frowned, raking a hand over his head, as he stared out at the waves. "So, here we are, talking about our days, and I have no idea what your usual kind of normal day could be."

The hesitation in his voice and melancholy in his eyes made River's heart lurch.

He snapped his fingers. "Say, I have an idea. Instead of going to the barbeque, why don't I spend some time at Watercolors?" He grinned. "Wouldn't Daphne just love that?"

The wrinkles of a frown tugged at her face. "Why would you want to do that?" Poor Daphne. She'd have a fit.

Again, he stared out at the water, gaze fixed on the revolving lighthouse beacon. He shifted his feet a couple of times and blew out more deep breaths. Finally, he shrugged. "I just realized I don't know what you do all day. Spending time with you would be a good way to get to know your business better."

She rolled around his answer. Was he genuinely interested in her life? Her pulse leaped at that suggestion. Or was he just nosy because it also affected his business now? She knelt to pet the terriers who had been patiently waiting for her attention. "I don't spend all day at Watercolors." She looked out at the lighthouse now. "I travel around town, talking to the business owners and residents. Sometimes, I collect their rent if it's due, and mostly, we talk about how we can improve business or property values. Or if something needs repaired, I make notes and then get it contracted out to be fixed."

He nodded. "All right. How many properties like that do you oversee?"

"Between the business and residential properties, thirty-nine locations."

He let out a low whistle. "All here in Sweetwater Harbor?"

She stood and bobbed her head.

"I see. How many are owned by my father?"

"You mean by you now? Twenty-eight, which does not count the vacant lands along the sound." River looked around, and her breath caught in her throat. They were alone on the beach. She could smell coffee on Calder's breath before the wind tore it away and see the shine in his blue eyes. How had they gotten so close? Why did they remain? Her pulse skipped ahead like waves rushing the shore during a storm. Heat unexpectedly invaded her body, shocking her. My word, she wasn't *into* Calder. Was she?

She needed distance so she turned for the stairs leading back to the house. "You know, I'm hungry. I think I'll go start dinner." Calling for the dogs, she headed indoors, away from the dropping temperatures and her rising reaction to his proximity. Inside the house, River hung up her jacket and scoured the kitchen for something for dinner. Again, she was in the mood for Thai. She'd tone down the spices a little this time, though. Maybe flaky egg tarts or steamed custard buns.

She curled her hands around the counter's edge and wondered what was happening. Why the sudden attraction to Calder? That shift toward him on the beach just now was eye opening, as was her body's unexpected, heated reaction to his suggestion he hang out with her for a day. She warmed inside like a July afternoon. Where had *that* come from?

Not finding an answer, she scooped up her hair, tied it, and pulled ingredients off the shelves. Only then did she notice her hands shook.

****

The next day River sat at her desk, absently twirling her pen in a circle. Her productivity shrank by the hour. She glanced at the phone, thinking of calling mom or Raine. No, she shook her head. No sense bothering them when she was just restless. Memories of walking the beach with Calder was not something she wanted to share with them. She moved a pair of manila files to another pile and rose. She needed coffee.

The front door of Watercolors opened, then closed with a clank. River dropped her coffee mug, jumping back as it smashed onto the tiled floor.

"Mercy, River!" Daphne rushed forward. "What happened?"

River fumbled and reached for the roll of paper towels. "I wasn't expecting you back so soon. You just took me by surprise." She ducked her head as she mopped up the broken shards and wet mess.

Except she'd been on high alert ever since getting to work today. Calder had not mentioned again whether he planned to join her at work. Once she left, she'd been anxiously wondering if he might stroll in. Rattled, and wondering why, and disgusted at herself because she was, she finished cleaning up the last of the mess. Now, as she stared at the floor, she wondered how she would survive the rest of the day. If only she could clean up the mess her mind and body had become as easily as she'd cleaned up the coffee mess.

Earlier, Daphne went out to run a few errands, and River prowled the office like a caged tiger, unable to concentrate on her computer screen or the figures before her. Giving up, she went in search of a few cookies and a cup of coffee. At least, the cookies survived. She wiped her hands and reached for another cookie.

Daphne set down the mail and her things, quietly regarding River. "Is that Calder Finn the one I should blame?" Her eyes narrowed.

"Calder has been the perfect house guest. I cannot complain one word about him."

Daphne nodded. "Then why are you as jumpy as a long-tailed cat standing beside a rocking chair?"

River grinned at the picture. That phrase was such an old cliché. "I didn't sleep well last night," she admitted, since it was true enough. "Guess I am just jittery." Which meant she certainly did not need any more caffeine.

"So, why didn't you sleep well?"

"The dogs were restless." True enough. Salty had gone to stay with Calder, and Pepper acted like she wasn't sure she liked having her buddy gone. "Maybe something was out on the beach?" She knew nothing had been out on the shore. She'd spent enough time looking at it under the moon light with Pepper last night.

"Right." Daphne returned to the mail.

River palmed three more cookies and headed to her office, in the desperate hope of getting something done. Daphne's expression looked far from convinced of her suggestion. Was she that transparent?

Hours later and calling it a day, she returned home

to change clothes for the beach dinner. Calder was nowhere around, and no note explained where he might have gone. Perhaps he was back at Frank's house, feeling a stab of disappointment he wasn't about to accompany her.

She peeled off her blouse and skirt and slipped into a bare-shouldered dress of soft pastels, accented by glittering rhinestones. Next, she exchanged studded heels for sequined ballet flats. Then she was ready, and hungry, for the beach. She scribbled a short note with the location, weighed it down with an apple on the counter, and grabbed her keys and a sweater.

The air was warm in the sound, heavily scented with yellow jessamine and firewheel. Swamp mallow was yet to bloom. Some of River's friends had already arrived and had a large bonfire burning on the sand for the barbeque and another fire for the huge kettle heating the gumbo.

Fewer houses sat along the sound, with its three short side streets spreading off the main trail running from the lighthouse to the end of the peninsula. This privacy afforded them lots of freedom.

Raine lived at the end of Sea Breeze Lane, the first lane north of the lighthouse. She promised she might pop in tonight.

Skirting the pot boiling the gumbo, River greeted her friends and helped to gather driftwood to add to the fires.

"Is your friend coming?" she was asked a couple times.

"I don't know. Maybe later," she answered, letting the matter drop. He knew the way if he chose to come. If not, maybe she'd bring him a plate. That would be the nice thing to do. Soon, she forgot about Calder as more friends came, including Raine, and someone produced a radio, filling the twilight beach with uplifting strands of drums, flutes, and guitars. The food was soon ready, and she took her place in line to fill her plate.

"Am I too late?" a voice whispered in her ear.

Whirling, she collided with Calder, his eyes twinkling as a smile crept over his face. "You made it." Suddenly she was acutely aware of the thumping in her chest, her tummy flipping, and rising heat sweeping through her inside.

"I did. Looks like my timing is rather good."

She nodded, moving up a step, drawing in a deep breath. "It is if you're hungry."

"I am."

That he would come if he were hungry seemed logical. His appearance didn't mean anything else except he was looking for a meal, and maybe some company to go along with. So why was her pulse racing just looking at him now, bathed in the glow of globe lights strung from the posts and the rising moonlight? Why was her body reacting and making more out of his presence? "Here." She handed over a plate, willing her hand not to shake this time.

Accepting it, he smiled.

Butterflies took off in her stomach, overriding her hunger.

Each person filled their plates with hot dogs, pimento burgers, and slawburgers cooked on the bonfire and a bowl of gumbo from the kettle in the sand and took their places next to Raine. Plastic cups of lemonade and sweet tea were passed out.

Eating took the pressure from talking. People exchanged notes on their day's activities, but conversation died down after that as they tackled their meals with newfound energies. As they were finishing, the music started back up again, softer strands this time. Flutes and saxophones joined in.

"You two should dance?" Raine asked, a crooked little grin teasing the corners of her mouth.

"Why would we do that?" River peeked at Calder and felt heat filling her face.

"No reason. I just wondered," Raine said as her friend came over, reaching for her hand. Nodding, she waved to her sister and Calder and stepped out onto the sandy dance floor.

"So, you didn't want to dance tonight?" Calder asked. He inclined his head to where Rained and her guy pal twirl around.

"I didn't say that." She took one last bite and set down her plate.

"You asked Raine why we would want to."

"I didn't say I want to," she corrected, "I asked why would we do that."

Sighing softly, Calder watched the half dozen dancers moving out onto the sand. "That's okay. I'm a bad dancer anyhow."

Finishing her tea, River considered Raine's question and Calder's comment. Was it just her or did he sound a little wistful as he watched them spin around the sand? Why would they dance? They certainly were not a couple. Yet, she invited him to come. He was here at her request…as a guest, a friend. But not *that* kind of friend.

So what exactly kind of friend was he? Sometimes

he could make her so mad, and at other times, she felt butterflies flapping somersaults through her tummy.

She chomped down painfully on her lip, jumped, and bit back an oath. She cut a glance at Calder.

He turned from the dancers to her, his dark brows raised.

She rose and reached for his hand. "Come on."

"What?" Blinking, he followed her. "What'd I just miss?"

She led him to a sandy spot and wrapped her arms around his neck. She pulled him close and breathed in his aftershave. "Just dance, Calder," she warned. She swayed to the music.

Gingerly resting his hands on the small of her back, he stared into her eyes. Unbidden, his hand moved up to wrap around the tangles in her hair, and he rubbed her locks between his fingers.

River felt herself slowly melting against his touch. A new, foreign but pleasant ache filled her. The feeling, and subsequent emotions, surprised her and strangely also excited her.

The full moon slowly rose like a disco ball above them, sparkling like rhinestones. The water washed up on the shore, the perfect accompanying melody for the soft music.

River closed her eyes, resting her head on Calder's shoulder. She moved her hands up to his hair. Fingertips spreading through his scalp, she tried to pull together a handful of his dark hair. She breathed in the wintergreen of his body wash, the mint of his toothpaste, and the woodsy musk of his aftershave.

Heat ignited between them, like the waves crashing ashore. They broke apart simultaneously, locked gazes for one second before moving forward as one, lips touching, plunging into a kiss of anticipation. She wanted his kiss so badly, her body cried out for it.

Fire and water washed over her, locking them and holding them still on the sand. Time stopped. White hot heat spiraled through her, and smoke rose between them.

Suggestions, promises, wishes, and desires passed between them in one long kiss. Finally, lungs bursting, they parted. She stood, dizzy, with his arms locked around hers. Was he as unsteady as she? River ran a tongue over her bruised lips, tasting the lemonade from his mouth.

"Wow," he whispered, breathless, licking his lips. "Berry lip gloss and sweet tea. You can kiss."

"Calder." She was surprised to hear the huskiness in her voice. "Just dance; don't talk." She briefly rested one fingertip to his lips before moving it to rest on his hip. Talking made her mad and got him into trouble. "I am doing this purely for pity."

Smiling, he took her into his arms once more. "Pity, huh?"

River hid her grin. As Calder held her, and she savored the new sensations his touch created, she recalled the words in Frank's poignant letter. Could these feelings and thoughts and emotions be what he had been talking about? How he wanted her to feel about love? If so, could he have possibly been referring to Calder?

The song finished, moving smoothly to the next one. River looked at Calder, and her chest tightened. His expression sat somewhere around expectant and hopeful, with his brows lifted into a V and his eyes wide and one corner of his mouth turned up as he waited to see her wishes on another dance. A chill slid over her as another thought struck her like a bolt of lightning. He was engaged to be married, to a woman who he did not love and who did not love him.

She had no business dancing with an engaged man or thinking the thoughts she'd been. Shame flooded through her. She inhaled, slammed a fist to her mouth, and stared in wide-eyed horror.

He gaped, drawing his brows together.

But she couldn't explain her thoughts. She shook her head and rushed back to her chair.

He followed, pressing a hand to her back. "What is the matter?"

Her physical reaction was the matter.

Chapter Ten

The next day, as the sun rose high in the sky, Calder returned to his dad's house and sat in the chair overlooking the bay. River was off walking along the beach, and if he tried hard enough, he suspected he could spot her. But right now he needed the distance, physical if nothing else. Their time spent at the beach party last night undid him in ways he was hard-pressed to label. Things were going very well, excellent even, until she withdrew with a horrified expression. She refused to answer his question of what was wrong, because he lacked the words, too.

Well, this place was his house now, for all practical purposes. But it would always be his dad's house. Just being inside it still unnerved him a little, but right now having the available respite also afforded him the more pressing luxury of distance. Where he wasn't tempted to hold River in his arms and kiss those bright, pouty lips again and wonder what suddenly horrified her. Talk about a smashing blow to his ego.

Keeping his gaze from straying to the ill-fated and unforgettable final spot where his dad lay, still soiled dull red on the floor, he studied the sunlight glinting off the water and the waves breaking onto the shore. What could he do?

He had to, at some point, wrap up things here and return to Atlanta. Once the law allowed him to, of course. That thought made him smirk. Brody could not keep running the business alone indefinitely, and of course, he was probably expected to be the groom at his wedding soon. Penelope might be a little upset if he failed to show. At least, he assumed she would notice.

He grinned. Her wrath was nothing in comparison to what he had seen from River so far. Her twists and turns, like her namesake, were beginning to bend his mind and heart in directions he never thought he would travel. Last night's beach party, and his body's and heart's reactions to River, scared him plenty. Then her dramatic reaction scared him even more. If only she would talk about it.

Just the thought of having to sit down with her, poring over ledgers and computer screens as they summarized his financial holdings here, sent more shivers squiggling down his spine. How could he be expected to be professional and attentive when all he wanted was to take her into his arms again and feel her silky hair and smell her herbal scents?

He stared at the harbor, where the water met the clouds, and looked for the answers to the questions in his mind. The gong of the clock made him jump, and he glanced at the timepiece on counter. Had he been locked in thoughts of River for half an hour? He must have lost track of the time. A quiet rapping at the door made him jump. Before he could rise to open the door, which he had failed to lock behind him, he heard the creaking of the hinges. He was developing bad habits, no doubt from being here for so long. He rose to see River's mother enter the living room. "Mrs. Gallagher, what a surprise."

"Calder, dear, I hope you don't mind me intruding

into your work."

Work? He almost laughed. "No, I am reflecting more than working today." He noticed how her gaze swept the room, settling on the stain on the floor. He also noticed how her fair skin blanched at the sight, and her lips thinned. "Is there something I can do for you?"

Shaking her head, she moved to the sofa and settled in. "No, dear. I just get bothered at times, you know. Frank was a great friend, as was your mother. And I suppose I still find his violent passing so hard to believe."

He nodded, blowing out a deep breath. "Me, too. And the local police have been so helpful." Sarcasm laced his tone. Short of jailing him and restricting his movements, they had done precious little in solving his dad's murder.

"In time, Calder, in time." Muriel patted her knees. "What are your plans?"

This time he did laugh, making a short, hollow sound. "I wish I knew."

She gave a shake of her head. "Perhaps the answers will become clearer in time as well, Calder. For the moment, would you and River consider joining us for dinner tonight? Cordell and I would love to have you both. Raine is coming as well."

Just what he needed. More time with the Gallagher clan. But the sincere hopefulness in her eyes ripped him. "What has River said?" he asked. "If she doesn't mind, I would be honored."

Muriel climbed slowly to her feet, resting a hand on his shoulder. "Wonderful, How about seven o'clock?"

"Fine." Somehow, he had the suspicion he agreed

to more than just a dinner.

"I'll let myself out. Don't worry so much about finding those answers," she suggested. "They might show themselves when you are least looking for them."

Wise advice, he supposed. Still, he felt the pressure of searching for them nonetheless. So River agreed they go for dinner at her parent's house? He could assume so. *Interesting.* Blowing out another deep sigh, he shifted his gaze back out to the sparkling waters and passing boats.

****

River stood on the sand, wind blowing her hair, salt on her skin, and her arms folded across her chest. Last night had been wonderful, sharing her time with friends—and Calder. Especially with Calder. No, she had not pitied him when she requested the dance. She pitied herself if anything, wanting to be held in his strong, warm arms. She wanted to be kissed by those lips. She found it tempting to yield to him, or did the spiraling heat inside her lie?

But he was already spoken for, and he was so set against her personal obligations for the town. That was one fact he reminded her of quite frequently and the engagement issue she reminded herself of. She allowed herself to forget he was engaged and instead indulged in how good he made her feel inside. He was slowly filling a void she had not known was there, and she was loving every second and wanting more of him. Until she remembered she could never have him.

Feeling like she was on a doomed voyage, she sought the isolation of the beach, needing to escape his very male and very hard-to-ignore presence in the house this morning. Not that he did anything wrong, he was just…there, easily upsetting her mental flow.

Screaming seagulls drew her attention up the beach, where her mom slowly made her way along the shore. Quickly, she stuffed her hands in her pockets and hastened to meet her, chasing sandpipers and plovers out of her way. "Mom, what are you doing here?"

"I came to see you."

"You could have called. I'd have stopped by. Is everything okay?"

Muriel flapped her arms at her daughter. "Pooh. Maybe I wanted to walk on the beach, too. Maybe I wanted to see you in person out here, not at the house. Everything is fine, so calm down, please."

Grinning, River settled, gaze going back to the water and boats and sea birds. Her mom would speak when she was ready. Together, they stood, arms wrapped about each other's waist and stared at the water. Assorted seabirds called, dipped, dove, and waded for their lunch around them.

"I remember all the times your dad, Lola, Frank, and I would spend out on the beaches here," Muriel said at length, her voice distant. "We walked, jogged, and combed for shells and oysters. We had bonfires and a few blowups."

The way her mom painted the scenes made River grin. The two families had been close. At least the parents had been, Calder really had truly little to do with her or her younger siblings. Maybe he had not liked the girls, and Winter had been too young.

"Lola and I were best of friends. I still miss her, nearly every day."

"I know you do, Mom. I miss her, too. And Frank, of course."

"Time is not always our friend. Sometimes, we stop and look around and realize we missed something or someone in our journey of life."

River's heart lurched, giving her a painful jolt. Had Frank's letter not suggested the same thing? So what did her mom think she was missing? Why did the thoughts echo the ones from last night? "Mom?"

Muriel blinked, looking over at River. "I want you to come to dinner tonight. Raine will be there. Bring Calder, too."

A houseful. "What's the occasion, Mom?"

Muriel gave a sigh. "Your dad and I have four children. Seems the twins are always out wandering someplace." She waved a hand at the sky and ocean. "But the other two are right here, close to home. Perhaps this business with Frank has made your dad and I realize we need to spend more time with our children while we can." She patted River's arm. "We don't want to die with the regrets Frank and Lola had with Calder."

Surprise filled her. She had no idea the Finns had regrets with Calder. What kind? Did her parents harbor regrets with her or the twins or Raine? Shame at herself and her siblings rose within her chest. "Of course I'll come, Mom. But do you really think Calder will intrude in what he will surely see as a family event?"

Muriel smiled. "We can only invite him and hope he will, now can't we? Don't you worry about him. Just bring yourself at seven tonight."

"Of course, Mom." Suddenly, she was looking forward to it. Besides, she didn't know if Calder could handle another of her Thai meals.

****

It was dinner time, and River was running behind to get ready. She hooked her bracelet as she swept into the living room and stopped short. "Well, don't you look nice?" She took in the scene before her.

Calder sat in the chair, Salt jumping toward his lap while Calder tried equally as frantic to keep the white dog off him. The pair looked comical.

Standing, Calder succeeded in brushing aside the dog. "White hairs on a dark suit will never do for dinner. The dinner invitation tonight requires the effort to look nice, sans doggie hairs," He dusted himself off. "Sorry, pal. As do you." He nodded at her outfit.

Suddenly, she pushed her hair aside, brushing it behind her ear, and then straightened her sweater. She usually never dressed up much for meals with her parents, but after talking to her mom, she felt the desire to. She'd selected a casual, yet attractive, outfit of worn, fitted jeans with a cropped, rhinestone bow sweater, and tasseled, shiny boots. All bling, of course. She'd left her hair down, loosely swishing. The fleeting memory of him playing with the locks last night still teased her. She studied him, her eyes narrowing.

He shifted. "I assume casual is fine."

Casual? A suit and tie was his notion of casual? He still wore one of his endless supplies of silly neck ties. She'd like to knot the whole bunch together and toss them into the ocean. "Do you mind?" She stepped close and slowly reached for him. For a moment, she met his gaze, questioning, then dropping to his neck.

She gently unknotted the tie at his neck and pulled it free of the collar. He sucked in a ragged breath, and she grinned. Next, she looped the fabric over her wrist, then released one button on his white oxford, allowing the collar to rest outside along the neckline of his sweater. Finished, she handed him the tie. "Casual," she said simply, turning away.

"Well, it's almost seven," he said. "Shall I drive us?"

Picking up her sweater, she turned and paused. A grin played on her lips. Had she just heard his voice crack?

****

Calder parked the car and glanced at the house, traveling his gaze the height of it before he glanced at River. What would happen tonight?

Raine was in the driveway, awkwardly wrestling an odd-shaped box from the back of her car. Seeing them exiting from Calder's rental, she flashed them both a smile. "Hi, guys. This is our dessert, but it's a little trickier than I thought."

Calder immediately stepped in. "Allow me." He slid his fingers under the carton. It felt light, but unbalanced. Adjusting for the balance, he nodded to the stairway. "Ladies first."

Flashing him another grin, Raine glanced at her sister and headed up, followed by River.

Muriel stood at the door. "Girls, Calder, don't you all look so nice," she stated. "Calder, that dessert can go on the kitchen counter, please."

He followed his nose down the hallway to the kitchen, where smells of cooking meat and other foods wafted into the air. His stomach grumbled. If he could handle a roomful of Gallagher women, he would no doubt have a wonderful meal. If he could handle the closeness of River next to him, he could no doubt be a saint.

"Storm called today," Muriel said over a dinner of roast beef and root vegetables. "She said she was heading over to track that series of thunderstorms and tornados happening in Oklahoma lately."

"I heard about them." Raine passed a plate of rolls around. "Supposed to be a forecaster's nightmare the way they keep popping up without reason."

Cordell set down his fork. "That is what makes Storm's work so valuable. The information she learns from those weather patterns and such will help scientists and the weather people better understand and predict the future storms. Hopefully enough so to save lives by early detection."

Calder listened, taking in Cordell's pride of his daughter's chosen career. Personally, he considered anyone who wanted to be out chasing storms to be absolutely insane. The dangers were enough to chill him to the bone. He also noticed the worry Muriel displayed about the present dangers and the obvious affection held by River and Raine for their wild-spirited sister. They were a close family, no doubt. Something quietly pricked him, but he waved it away.

"Winter sent a message, as well. He is due for a break shortly. He did not mention what he had been doing lately, just that he was safe and hoping to come home soon." Muriel smiled.

The atmosphere instantly changed to one of relief.

Interesting, that the twins who had been born in the middle of a blizzard apparently lived for thrills in their lives now. Interesting. When had River been born? Suddenly, he found himself more curious about that question than the conversation of the other Gallagher children. Unfortunately, he had not spent enough attention while growing up alongside them to recall any mentions of birthdays. Surely, his mother had baked goodies or taken a gift. So, why didn't he recall ever attending a single party? Apparently, it was one more in the long string of opportunities he had lost out on while living here.

He would make a point to ask River when her birthday was at the first chance he had. Unexplainably, he had to know. Now that he was dwelling on it, what else had he missed while living next door to these people? As much as he had missed while living with his parents? That niggling thought persisted, pricking him again, like the words in his dad's letter.

"Calder, I just can't get over how you have matured," Muriel said, hands on her chin. "You look so successful."

Heat rushed to his face, and he ducked his head. "Thank you," he murmured.

She looked around the table, sighing deeply. "Seems like just yesterday you were all so young and had such grand dreams. Lola and I listened to each of your fantasies, wishing each one came true. You all wanted fame and fortune, and we added love and health, of course."

"Yes, of course." More words from his dad's letter returned. "We have all succeeded to some extent, no doubt thanks to so many well wishes."

"Your parents talked about you what seemed like every day for months after you left," Muriel waved a hand. "Lola shared each letter and phone call in great detail, because they meant so much to her."

He wasn't keen that his letters and calls had been made public. He tried to ignore it, but River's amused stare across the table was impossible to overlook, and he was hard pressed not to squirm. The meat, though succulent and juicy, turned to dried leather in his mouth.

"Calder, care to join me out back while the Muriel and the girls set up?" Cordell asked as they were wrapping up the roast. "If I know my baby, Raine's dessert might take a moment to unpack."

Raine huffed at her dad but smiled and blushed. "This recipe is a new blend I am working on. You all are my guinea pigs tonight."

Calder wasn't sure he liked the sound of that, but the rest of the clan did not seem to mind. He was glad for the escape, however temporary, from Muriel's reminiscing and River's amusement.

Cordell scraped his chair and shuffled out to the back porch. He sat in a cushioned Adirondack chair and pulled a pipe from his pocket. Lighting it, he took a long puff and looked out toward the ocean waves.

A fishing vessel, decked out in lights, chugged into port, its whistle blowing. Sea birds rushed through the shallows. Seated opposite Cordell, Calder waited, cradling his wine glass, smelling the tobacco and thinking of holding River on the beach the night before.

"Your dad and I were out here, sitting and smoking and talking, just last month, son." Cordell talked around his pipe. "Your dad loved a good pipe, too, on occasion."

Really? He never knew that. Since when? The unintentional name "son" rocked him a little, especially used in the same sentence about his dad.

"He knew he didn't have much time left, and he was mostly reminiscing about you and Lola. He was devastated when you left town, they both were, but he understood how important building your career was."

Calder bit back a cringe. He had no idea his leaving hit his parents so hard. Because he had been in too big of a hurry to get away. From what?

"Seems the Gallagher and the Finn families both left Ireland about one hundred and fifty years ago, or thereabouts, and drifted to this area eventually," Cordell continued. "My grandfather was the first who left Ireland and sailed to America when he was a lad. Landed in New York and began walking south, his intention was to see as much of America as he could. Story goes he somehow broke his leg when he got to the North Carolina coast and was laid up a spell. By the time he healed, he had fallen for one of the local lasses and never left. He wrote back home to the rest of the family and over time, others joined him."

Cordell pointed out over the ocean and clouds. "I guess the lapping waves, salt air, and cooler temperatures reminded them of their native coastal towns. Your mom and dad were the youngest generation to leave Ireland directly. The Finn family hailed from Counties Sligo and Galway and the Gallagher clan from Counties Donegal and Mayo. They took wives and raised families. Sweetwater Harbor has been a treasured home to the Gallaghers and Finns for many decades, son. We have become content in our old years."

The content comment pierced him, reminding him painfully of his dad's letter. Sitting out here with Cordell Gallagher was like sitting down to read his dad's letter again. Content versus complacent. So, where exactly was he residing lately?

Not liking the answer, he shifted his thoughts over to the history lesson Cordell gave him. Most of it was old news and most importantly, River was the current generation determined, with bulldog fierceness when necessary, to keep the town as it has been for decades. He leaned forward, taking a whiff of the bitter tobacco smoke. "But honestly now, how long can the town hope to survive locked in the decades-old mind set?"

Cordell withdrew his pipe, tipping his head to one side. "Just as long as there is a new generation content to keep it that way."

In other words, indefinitely if people like River come along. Sighing, he leaned back, clasping his hands behind his head. His town, and what the blue blazes could he do with it? What he once foolishly envisioned as a largely joyous and rewarding opportunity turned into a headache of major proportions. Life was supposed to be just about the money. So, when had it turned into being about the feelings?

He looked out over the water, where gulls and sea birds cried, and the boats chugged, and clouds danced across the horizon. The scene was peaceful, but it made him curl his fists as his chest tightened. Why did he even care about feelings? When had he ever let feelings get in the way of finances? Certainly not when he was in Atlanta.

"Look, son, I know you have a hard path to follow. I recall you as a teen, bursting at the seams to get away. I know you have recently been handed a lot, and my daughter is not making your life any easier." He paused, chuckling. "But the truth is, son, you could be doing a lot worse right now."

Calder blinked. "How do you figure that?" He could count the problems and inconveniences beset him since his arrival and run out of fingers...and toes, as well. Surely old Cordell Gallagher was going daft too. Must come from dealing endlessly with Gallagher women. Perhaps he needed to take a lesson from Cordell regarding River.

"Son, if I have to explain it to you, you aren't half as smart as we all thought you were." He slapped the armrest. "You aren't daft or slow, are you?"

"Not normally," he slowly responded as indignation rose through the sinking feeling in his chest. What was this place doing to him?

"All right, are you guys ready for the inside-out cake?" Muriel came to the doorway.

"Inside-out cake? What is that?" Calder lifted himself from the chair. Already he was looking past Muriel and hoping for a glance of River.

"It's Raine's most current design. You know she is quite the baker, right?"

"So I've been told."

"She delights in creating new flavors and whatnot. We are the willing test subjects before they are offered to the public at her bakery."

Again, he wasn't sure he liked being a test subject, but supposed Raine would never endanger her family, so he must be safe enough. He found River inside, setting out fresh plates and forks. The sun, slowly setting in the window beyond her, shone through and hit her hair, setting it aflame with a brilliant glow. Head bent to her task, she softly hummed to a tune only she could hear, and a satisfied smile played on her lips.

The sight and sound were enough to ground him to

the spot, driving any sense of reason from his mind. Spellbound, he could only stare. His mouth went dry. Words from his dad's letter drifted back, wrapping around him with silken ropes.

Task complete, she looked up. "Calder, do you need more wine?"

Her question, so innocently asked, sent rockets of confusion and electricity through him. Her smile lit him up inside.

He'd forgotten the now-empty glass in his hand. Loosening his grip on the stem, he stared at the glass. "Yes, I suppose more would be good." Or something a lot stronger than wine.

She twisted around, reaching for the wine bottle. "Raine makes the best desserts." River poured the red liquid into the glass. "Do you have a sweet tooth?"

"A little, yes," he replied while she poured the wine. "When is your birthday?" he blurted, feeling heat touch his face when she looked his way. Her eyes rounded, and he barely suppressed the urge to run his hand under his collar.

"It's April fifteenth. I'm a tax baby."

Slowly, he caught the connection. Suddenly, a million things that he did not know about her popped into his mind. What was her favorite color? He'd bet Thai was her favorite food group. Terriers might be her favorite type of dog, but what was her favorite movie? Book? Unexplainably, he wanted to know all those little details now. Why had she looked at him with such a horrified expression last night?

He followed her to the dining room where Raine and her mother set up the cake.

Cordell stared, frowning. "Where's the icing? Did

you forget it, girl?"

Raine giggled. "No, Daddy, it's inside the cake. Inside out, remember?"

Calder lifting one eyebrow toward the yellow cake, confirming Cordell's doubting opinion. The cake did rather look like a half-finished project that someone forgot to ice. "What's with the green stuff?"

"Leaves. The others are flower petals. They are both completely edible. Just a little different in lieu of the traditional icing." Raine smiled.

Calder thought she looked like a proud mother showing off her baby as she glanced from her cake to those seated around the table.

Of course. Like with her sister, Raine's explanation left something to be desired. No matter. They were discussing dessert. River and he tackled much weightier things, like property and money.

Once they were all seated again, Raine doled out the slices.

River dove in, her sweet tooth evident, and clearly excited at a new sample to try. The lemon cake was moist and spongy. Inside were the surprise layers of chocolate buttercream icing and the vanilla crème filling.

"You baked them with the cake. How clever, Raine," Muriel praised between big bites. "What other flavors do you think you might do?"

Raine waved her fork. "I was thinking of a chocolate cake with either devil's food icing or whatever. I can mix up any traditional cake and icing flavor."

"Calder, what's your favorite sweet flavor?" River asked suddenly, looking over at him.

"Key lime is good, I suppose. Pumpkin pie is nice. I really am not picky."

Cordell pushed aside his empty plate and patted his stomach. "Very good, Raine, my dear. Another smashing success." He looked around the table, stopping at Calder and River. "I think tomorrow is supposed to be a pleasant day. Why don't the two of you go out on the boat?"

Calder tightened his grip around the fork. *Boat*? Cordell wanted him to step onto a boat. With River? What could possibly go wrong?

Chapter Eleven

Calder supposed this day was the picture-perfect ideal for a boater. Sunlight sparkled off the water in the bay. The *Wind Quest* bobbed gently on its mooring line. Fisherman loaded their gear to make ready for a day's work. Sea birds called and swooped. Plovers and sandpipers dashed along the sandy shore. The smell of fish was overpowering.

River hummed as she did various things to prepare the boat.

Waiting on the dock, Calder watched. He was seasick already, and they hadn't even left port.

"Ready?" She motioned for him to cross over. Her smile was bright, showing her happiness.

He nodded, swallowed, sucked in a breath, and hoped for the best. Considering he'd spent his first eighteen years living in a coastal town, he'd never been comfortable around boats. He suffered through them when he absolutely had to and asked for no more.

Cordell told him this cabin cruiser was River's baby and something she enjoyed doing, so by thunder, he would enjoy it with her. Even if this little daytrip suggestion of Cordell's killed him, which he figured was not outside the limits of expectation.

Crossing over, he misstepped and stumbled. Immediately River caught him, curling her hand around his wrist, and lending him her own body to balance on.

Their gazes met. His heart fluttered as her lips parted and her blue eyes slightly widened. Was he going to kiss her again? He wanted to, and the question was clear in her expression. In that instant, he was glad for this little journey. The idea of the two of them, at sea together, sounded altogether cozy. The little firecrackers shooting off inside him proved his intense attraction.

The boat bobbed again on a wave.

River retreated, a hand going to her throat.

He'd bet the intense attraction was mutual, or the blush on her cheeks lied. Except her doe eyes seemed haunted today. He supposed haunted was a step up from horrified.

"Well, uh, welcome aboard." She donned her white captain's cap. "Do you want to ride up here with me?" She motioned toward the cockpit.

"Sure." Why not? He could be tempted to kiss those rounded lips just as easily as standing beside her. Somehow, he knew this journey would shake him in ways he could only imagine right now. He also had to acknowledge her skill in boating. Like most things lately, he'd been too quick to misjudge her.

****

Coasting out of the marina, River turned her boat into open water. Relaxing into the task, River closed her eyes, drinking in the sunshine and ocean wind, and feeling the engine's rumbling power beneath her feet. Boating was truly a passion that one had to experience to fully appreciate.

Popping open one eye, she peered over at Calder. He still gripped the console but at least he wasn't as green as he'd been back on the dock. How had he lived here for all those years and never acquired an appreciation for boating? "So, what do you think?"

"Good. Great. Fun."

She smiled at the pauses between each answer. "Dad had a great suggestion, didn't he?"

He nodded.

"See those clouds?" She pointed overhead. "They are cirrus clouds. Storm told me all about the clouds and various formations last time she and I took out the *Wind Quest*. Cirrus clouds are good clouds."

He shook his head. "I never knew there could be bad clouds."

"Storm's terminology. Probably not a technical or real term. Cirrus clouds can indicate good weather conditions. The dark storm clouds, like cumulonimbus, are an indication of bad weather."

"Tell me more about Storm and Winter." He loosened his grip, relaxed, and leaned back in the upholstered chair. "How'd she get into all that storm chasing stuff to begin with? Don't you all feel it's an absolutely dangerous and crazy career choice?"

River grinned. "Maybe a little, but she is careful. She has a team, and they all look out for each other. After Winter enlisted in the army, Storm enrolled at the university inland. She started out studying meteorology, thinking to be a meteorologist or something like that. She volunteered one year to help storm spot. One thing led to another, and eventually she became a full-time storm chaser. She's one of the few that makes a decent living. She's been all over and has been awarded loads of research grants."

"Interesting. I had no idea it could be so technical."

"Hey, check out that boat." She watched as his

attention focused at an on-coming craft. She curled her fingers tightly around the wheel and narrowed her gaze at the boat. "Reckless idiot," she murmured. "The driver isn't following any of the rules for ocean engagement."

"I hadn't known there was such a thing…rules for engagement."

"There is. All boaters learn them before piloting a craft. Just like learning to fly a plane. The driver is probably a real amateur judging by the way they are driving. If they keep those stunts up, they might swamp a smaller craft. In fact—oh! They're coming straight at us. Hold on!" Leaning toward him, she cranked the wheel, pulling the boat sharply through the water.

"It changed directions to stay with us." Calder pointed, as his jaw dropped at the driver's sheer audacity. "What's wrong with that driver?"

"I don't know, but I don't like it," she panted. She yanked on the wheel again, plowing her boat through the waters. "Okay, fun's over; time to go back."

Soon, the harbor and lighthouse came into view. Just as River thought she would make it, and she could report the crazy driver to the harbormaster, a shot rang out. Spinning, her pulse jumped. "That was a gunshot!"

Calder clamped his palms on her shoulders, pushing her down. "Yes, and it was aimed at us. Get down."

She pushed him away. "I can't see to drive."

"You can't see to drive if you're dead either."

River went to her knees, staying up just enough to see over the wheel. Who in the world would be shooting at her and Calder? A thought struck her, and she chilled, inhaling sharply.

"Do you think that's whoever killed Frank?"

The stony look in his eye shot more chills arcing off through her. He'd already concluded that very real probability. Someone was out to kill them next.

The next shot echoed, piercing the side of the *Wind Quest.* River twisted, squealing in anger.

"Down!" Calder commanded.

"That moron shot my boat!" She shoved aside his hands and peered at the damage. It would not be enough to sink them but sufficient to leave a sizeable hole in the polished wood. Her body tightened and her breath caught as rage ripped through her.

"He or she was aiming at us." Calder pointed out. "Now, down. And why aren't you driving us to port?"

"No way. This is war." She ignored his question, scrambled to her feet, and snatched the wheel. With her teeth clenched, River leaned on the wheel, bringing the boat sharply about again. She pushed the throttle, sending it forward with a mighty lurch.

"So, is this the angry part?" Calder asked from his spot down on the boat's deck.

"What?"

"You once told me I'd know the difference between when you're upset and when you're really angry. I wonder if this might be the angry part because your eyes are narrowed, your teeth are gritted, and your hands are clenched around the wheel. If these details all added together aren't angry, I couldn't imagine what is."

"Of course I'm angry!" She fixed her gaze on the approaching boat. "Wouldn't you be? How can even think of stuff like that right now?" She dragged the wheel again and raked her hair out of her face. "Call for help if you have reception. My phone won't work out here."

"Don't you have ship-to-shore radio or anything like that?" He fished out his cell phone and sucked in a deep breath.

"I'm just a little busy right this minute." Yes, she could tell her teeth were clenched tight. So was her chest.

"Oh no. I've only got two bars. Hopefully, that will be enough."

River cringed at the dismay in his voice, though she silently commended him for his composure so far. She watched as he dialed and heaved a sigh when someone evidently picked up.

He explained their situation. "There! Another shot. Did you hear that?" he shouted into the phone. "That driver is out to get us!"

"Hang on," River cautioned, gaze still locked on the other boat. "This ride will get—" Her words slacked off as she violently spun the wheel at the last moment, abruptly cutting off the other boat and forcing it to turn. The two bows missed each other by mere feet. "Rough. Grab something," she said. "The wake might be choppy." Whatever smooth sailing she experienced was now gone.

Strong waves and an uneven wake sent Calder's phone sailing from his hand and clattering across the deck. "Oh no. Hopefully they got our location. All I could tell them was in the middle of the Atlantic Ocean."

"Okay, let's see what else they have," River spat out.

"You're not doing that again, are you?" Calder

could not hide the dread in his voice.

"Of course I am. That blasted idiot shot at us. I have a hole in my boat now. What if it is the same person or people who killed Frank? They are not getting away. Even if we have to stick with them halfway to Europe."

"You're not ramming this boat into that one, are you?"

"No. If I did, we'd both go down. I just want to get their attention."

"You sure have mine, and I assume you have theirs, too. Whoever it is, they surely didn't expect you to turn and head straight for them."

She gave a tart smile. "I do like the element of surprise."

"I recall that. I need to say this, though it might be completely inappropriate right now. But I'd like to say, just in case we sink or get shot or somehow don't make survive."

"Calder, we'll make it through." She brought the boat about as another gunshot rang out.

He ducked and yanked on her leg. "As I was saying, River, I must admire your plucky anger, especially since it's finally not aimed at me. You take my breath away with how you stand straight and tall and make a fantastic target at the wheel."

At his less-than-subtle point, she smirked.

"In another era, you might have made a fantastic lady pirate. Right now you make a fine warrior." He cringed as another gunshot ricocheted off the side of the boat. "I just thought you should know that. Before we join the fish at the bottom of the sea."

"We're not sinking, okay? I'm touched at your

words, most of them anyway." She swerved the boat again, water arcing out behind them. "Thanks, but I intend to survive and find out who that maniac is."

"I'd like to know who it is, too. Can't we just wait for the police to get here?"

"And be a sitting duck?" She laughed. "No thank you."

The boats roared through the waves, exchanging wakes as they crisscrossed each other.

"I feel like we're just playing a giant game of chess all over the water."

"I'm not playing."

Another shot ricocheted. "I doubt they are either."

River closed in enough to make out a single occupant in the boat. "It's a woman. And she's got her gun up, pointed at us again. Shoot at me and my boat, witch!" She grated, pushing the throttle. "Hang on."

Calder grabbed her by the waist, yanking her down. "Get down here. She's shooting again!"

"I have to get to the wheel!" She slapped away his hands.

"You'll get that pretty, stubborn head blown off. Now, down." He wrapped his arms around her and tightened his jaw against the strain as she fought to pull free.

"She'll sink us!"

Fighting for control, he wrestled for her hands. "Between the two, I'll take sinking over getting shot."

"Coward." Wrestling free with a heavy grunt, she lunged for the wheel again. "She's coming close. I can see her face."

"Okay, so who is trying to kill us?"

River had to grin at the curiosity that had him on

his knees, peering at the person steering the boat like a crazy drunkard. She watched the look of sheer incredulous shock wash over him.

"Penelope?"

River spun at his disbelieving croak. "Your fiancée?"

"The world had just come apart at the seams."

Her heart twisted in sympathy at his bewildered expression and hollow words. Now, she was curious. "What is your fiancée doing out here, shooting at us?"

"I have no earthly idea." He could only stare.

River shoved his head as she turned the wheel to the right as the woman fired off another shot. "I'm sorry, but I don't care who she is. I just know what she is doing now. Her intention seems clear to me. And don't forget what she might have done to Frank."

"Can't you just outmaneuver her until help arrives? Can't you just drive us back to shore?"

"Every time I circle toward shore, she cuts me off, and I can't dodge bullets indefinitely."

Calder sank to the deck, his shoulders drooped, and he stared at his upturned palms in slack-jawed angst.

River's heart ached for his crestfallen surprise and pain. She wished she could drop down to the deck and give him a hug, and she considered just that. He stared at his empty hands as if the answers to the last few minutes were written there.

Another shot ricocheted off the boat, and heat seared through her. With teeth clamped, she bore down on her opponent. Calder's fiancée! Well, what a surprise! Dozens of questions filtered through her mind as she steered the boat, wary of the gun pointed her way. Questions that would have to wait.

Another shot barked, echoing, and slamming into the hull of the *Wind Quest*.

"She better have good insurance to pay to fix my boat." Unless she succeeded and took the boat down, she and Calder with it. She cast a fast look at Calder and decided he was the most miserable and shocked man she had ever seen...and angry. She smiled at the anger she could see slowly simmering beneath his fear and surprise.

Sirens wailed.

She looked around. Two police cruisers sliced through the water, heading for them with their blue lights swirling. She and Calder just might survive yet. Emboldened by the fact help was close by, she gunned the throttle once more, steering the boat toward the woman.

Seeing the police boats charging over the waves, Penelope lowered her gun, using both hands to escape.

"Oh no," River yelled and waved a fist in the air. "No way are you getting out of this now." Turning the wheel, she cut the other boat, forcing her to slow down.

The police boats stormed close, one coming alongside each vessel. Officers in uniform swarmed aboard, barking orders and demanding answers.

"Her!" River pointed. "She shot at us. Just look at my boat!"

Calder watched, hands clenched, as Penelope's gun was discovered.

Frisked, she was handcuffed and taken over to the police cruiser. Turning her head, she ignored Calder and River.

"We will follow them back to the dock." River gently rested her hand on his shoulder. She doubted he heard a word the police or she said in the past few moments. He'd been too busy staring at his fiancée, his face a myriad of confused emotions.

She considered driving Calder back to the house, brewing a pot of herbal tea, and comforting him with a huge mug. Green tea? Lemongrass? Chamomile? Poor guy looked about ready to collapse to the weathered boards.

****

Once they reached the marina, Calder and River crossed over to the dock.

While River secured her damaged boat and spoke to the police, Calder placed himself before Penelope, taking her jaw into his cupped hand and bringing up her gaze to face him. The sheer, bitter coldness glaring from those eyes shook him to his core. His knees shook, surprising him. His heart thumped heavily, and his palms were slick. He wiped them on his pants.

"Penelope." He licked his dry lips. "Can you explain any of this...?" Words failed him. He coughed and tried again. "I don't understand. What are you doing here? How did you find us on the boat?"

She sneered, jerking free of his hold. "You are a fool. I've been following you all through this seedy, little, miserable smudge of a town for three whole days. I've seen how you've made a fool of yourself over that woman."

He stood; his thoughts whirled at her bitter words. Had he been so blind? He wrestled with her words and her accusations. "I don't understand why you are here. Why aren't you in Atlanta, planning the wedding?"

"I am planning, but not our wedding." She smiled brightly. "This action was my clever plan to get your fortune."

Mystified, he shook his head. Nothing made any sense. One of them was not fully in control of their right mind, and right now he wasn't sure who it was. "But once we're married, it's mostly yours anyway. Why all the planning? Why shoot at River and me?"

"Only half is mine as your wife. But with you locked away for life for murder, I get it all as your surviving spouse. Plus I would have also gotten this miserable little town as your inheritance from your father. I could do so much with this dot on the map once it's leveled down to the ground."

"I still don't understand." Calder tried to wrap his mind around her angry words and her burning eyes, so far removed from the socialite he'd proposed to. She was already set to inherit a sizeable fortune from her parents. True, it had to be shared with her siblings. What had he missed? Her confession was a verbal slap across the jaw, stinging his soul.

"By ensuring you went to prison for a life term, I get all of my fortune and yours. Enough clues would be presented later, after we were married but before we could have children, to surface and implicate you for your father's murder."

So, she would not have even children of her own to share any wealth with? "You killed my father? You're the one who murdered him and trashed the house? And you planned to pin it on me." The cold facts might have hurt him less if she wasn't so smug about them. Even now, under arrest, she retained her socially superior air. He once found that confident presumption amusing. Now he found it nauseating. He almost heaved as his stomach churned. Seeing the hatred in her eyes, he swallowed the hollow disbelief.

"Yes. I called the police from down the road, saying I was jogging by and heard two men arguing. I gave them your description."

Now he knew why they arrested him on sight. He took a step back, revolted at her smug tone. Now he understood the exact feeling of getting framed. He spread his palms, making one last appeal. "He was dying, Penelope. Dying from cancer! He did not have much longer. Did you have to beat and kill him that way, too? I mean…" Words utterly failed him. He swept his glance out to the water as he swallowed the bile churning in his gut. He looked back and wondered how he missed all the clues pointing to her diabolical tendency.

She shrugged. "He asked for it."

River, having stood by and listening, surged forward, a battle cry on her lips. She raised her hands and launched through the air.

Calder caught her, pinning her arms, feeling her hot anger slamming against him. The brute force took away his breath.

"I will personally see you rot forever in the darkest, coldest prison cell there is, witch!" She clawed against Calder to get to Penelope.

"Take her away," Calder murmured and turned from Penelope. Angry retorts and promises of her return followed, but he only heard River's breathless promises of revenge. Whirling her around, he dropped his lips onto hers, plunging his tongue deep into her mouth. He captured her waist, pressing her close. He reached to ensnare her hair and slowly released her.

Breathless, with her lips red, she glared, her eyes

dancing. "Are you always this impetuous?"

He looked around the marina, at the boats and inhaled the smelly stench of fish caught by the weathered old men. All sights and sounds from his childhood when he wanted to be anywhere but here in town. Now, he couldn't imagine being anywhere else.

He looked back at River, and he saw only her wild beauty. Suddenly a laugh bubbled up within him. Absurd, this situation also felt so right. Like being here in Sweetwater Harbor suddenly made him feel completely whole. Why had he ever thought he wanted to go away? Yes, in that regard, Penelope was right: he was a terrible fool, about so many things.

"Not normally." He laughed again and brought her close. "But it's such a wonderful life we can have, and I just can't help it."

Sure he was losing his mind, he chuckled again. "River Gallagher, I know this is terribly fast, but will you marry me? I promise you we won't change a thing about this dear old town."

****

Calder and River relaxed poolside, soaking in the late afternoon sunshine. She looked up from one of the endless lists she was forever working on and smiled. Her warm smile sent a shiver of hot delight up his spine.

"Okay, let's see." She moved a fingertip back to the list. "We have to invite the cousins, too."

Calder lifted an eyebrow. "Cousins? You mean there's more Gallaghers?"

River smacked him on the arm with her notepad. "Of course, there are more. You are marrying into a big family now."

He rubbed his arm and grinned. "I am looking forward to lots of things coming from being married to you. A big family was just one more plus."

Three days had passed since the boating episode, and each one of them was needed to finally convince her to marry him. Her uncanny ability to utterly confound and yet enchant him reminded him very much of his father's letter. He now took solace from the thought that somewhere beyond the known, his parents watched, smiling in happiness.

Now she'd finally said yes, she had not stopped making plans. Or producing relatives. "Okay," he said with an exaggerated sigh. "The cousins."

"Yes, on Mom's side mostly. A few on Daddy's, too. There's Summer, Autumn, Brooke, Rumor, Chance, and Honor. Now, Winter already said he could be here since he has a bunch of leave time saved. So that just leaves Stormie." Her voice trailed off as she nibbled a fingernail.

Calder pulled her hand, curling his fingers around hers. His lips grazed her knuckles. "Tell me more about Storm. How do you think we can get her word if she is out in some remote location on the run?"

"Oh." She shrugged. "Mom always manages somehow."

"That doesn't surprise me. Muriel Gallagher is a very capable woman, as are her daughters."

River smiled. "Of course, getting her to come is another story."

Calder started. "Certainly she'd come to her own sister's wedding?"

"She will want to. But she's wild. She loves to chase those storms. If one pops up at the same time, we'd be in competition to it."

Calder ran his tongue slowly along her knuckles, chuckling as she giggled and squirmed. Ticklish? One more thing he couldn't wait to learn about River. "Storm can't be anywhere near as wild as you. I'll never forget your fury out on the boat. I've never seen anyone so angry and so beautiful and so wild."

River laughed. "I'm ticklish!" She wriggled away.

He lunged, pinning her to the towel.

She reached out her hand and scooped some pool water at him.

"Hey!" Shivers swept over him.

Beside him, River shivered and went still.

Instantly, he stopped all kidding and draped another towel over her. "Are you okay?"

"Yes, fine." She sat up and arranged the cloth like a royal robe. I was just thinking of your dad's letters. And then the wind blew across like destiny."

He tilted a brow. "Like destiny?"

"Yes, your dad talked about destiny and a journey, remember? He was right; it was certainly well worth it."

"You mean I'm well worth the journey?" At the thought, he grinned.

She shrugged, her grin spreading wide. "Yes, you are most definitely worth any journey."

His chest probably swelled two sizes. He dropped a kiss on her nose. "I agree. The last week or so has been awesome. Because you're in my life. Now, tell me about Storm and storms competing."

River shrugged. "Oh, Storm is way wilder than me; just ask Mom or Dad. She has a terrible temper and is very independent. She can be hard for us to handle."

Calder bit back a grin. River's description of her sister sounded very much as though she were describing herself. If this next sister were even more like that, he felt bad for any guy who met her face to face and had to deal with her wrath. She sounded like a real force to be reckoned with. He wouldn't wish that sort of wild woman on any man.

On second thought, he wondered what Brody would think about a woman like that. He would bet a dozen donuts that Brody would run far and fast if he ever met a woman like River just described Storm to be.

A word about the author...

Ryan Jo Summers lives in Western North Carolina where she draws inspiration for her fiction stories. She has had over a dozen fiction novels, novellas or anthology inclusions published since 2012. Several of her previous works have been nominated by industry and peer reviewed awards. She also writes non-fiction articles and essays for local, regional, and national magazines, devotionals, and trade journals.

She enjoys cooking, gardening, reading, painting, and enjoying birds and nature, or simply gathering with friends. She is an animal advocate and likes to foster unwanted pets for area rescue organizations.

Visit her at:

http://www.ryanjosummers.com

Thank you for purchasing
this publication of The Wild Rose Press, Inc.

For questions or more information
contact us at
info@thewildrosepress.com.

The Wild Rose Press, Inc.
www.thewildrosepress.com